Betrayal and Its Scars

Greta Bonati

*'I let my thoughts unravel,
my shrieking unseen, unforetold
I let my mouth demolish my reputation,
my bigger ego
I let my ears haunt me, taunt me, tease me,
Till I find myself tormented to tears
in the corner...'*

Prologue

Dearest diary,

It's the eighty-ninth day on which I find myself awoken by the unbearable blow of gunshots and the monstrous roars of explosions. Trees blasted from the ground like fireworks in a summer night sky. People perish second after second like dominoes in a spiral, till none remain standing. Us in orange, hidden between trees, representing our mantra: balance and stimulation. The purple's on top of Mount Rore, representing theirs: power and ambition. They are the enemies, or so I am told. But aren't we all? Aren't we all enemies, one to another? I'm as much a stranger to my leader as I am to my enemy. Out in the yonder fields, dirt and powder and ashes carpet the once-vivid green grass. The vicious gray clouds torment the once so light and airy sky. Where is the life?

I hear commands approach my ear, an indication to exit the bunker. I take my usual spot behind a rock and wait to shoot. Until the sun goes down and the crickets start to sing. The cold and the wind keep me company in this deadly place, as I tally-mark another week on my counting stone. It's another week which has flown by. Tomorrow signifies ninety days since the war has begun, which indicates that it will no longer be a routine, but rather a habit. This life, filled with death and destruction, is my life. Nonetheless, for now, I place my thoughts to the back of my mind, and do my duty.

It's barely hours till nightfall, when I realize a white flag slices the air, like a shark parting the water in a vast, navy, ocean. It only took me a matter of seconds to see that there was not one, but two white flags, flapping in the devouring air. How can this be? Moreover, what does it mean? Has the war finally terminated? Can I go home to my family, to my friends? I yearn so dearly for it all to cease. I decide to climb out from my spot behind the rock, and watch as my leader, and the opposing side's leader shake hands, peacefully. Surely, it's a good sign!

I thought I couldn't be happier, until they started patting one another on the back, and exchanging words. This was the most content I've been in a really, really long time. Ophelia, you made your way back to our bunker where you would soon inform us all on what had just occurred. 'It's over!' you had begun saying. 'We have won! We all have won! We can go home; our job is done! The land will be shared amongst our countries!' you said in the biggest of smiles I had ever seen in my entire life. It just seemed so unreal, yet it felt better than a dream. We all started cheering and laughing, crying too. The days of foolish hunger in the pit of our stomachs were over! The days of cold, parched skin on our feeble bodies will never keep us up late at night again! The days filled with the witnessing of traumatic sins being committed will haunt us no more. I felt so relieved. As if a wave ran me over, stroked me, and left, with all my displeasure along with it. Leaving me clean, innocent. Humble even. I hastily picked up the last of my belongings, as I exited the bunker for the very last time.

As I step outside, I remain shocked to the bone, as chills and goosebumps take control over my every system. All around me, rose red petals swim gracefully through the atmosphere. They penetrate through the furious gray clouds, they shower the fallen, beaten trees and finally, gently hover, caressing the ashes and dirt and powder which contaminates the below. There are just no words to describe it all. The simple acknowledgment of freedom. Such a small word for such a powerful and incredible sensation. I feel refreshed, nourished and better yet, I'm feeling at my highest, knowing I haven't killed a single soul in all my life.

Lots of love, my dear,

Arthur.

Chapter one

Who am I anymore?

Bloop Bloop, ah there goes the last of the marshmallows. I place my now-cold mug onto the floor, where the pre-existing circular mark remains. After all, it's always the same: the same old view, trees and trees of one kind, pine. The same night patrol still consists of the same cranky employees, the stars. The same squeaky chair, rocking back and forth in the darkest hours of the day. The same floor, adorned with only the peanut colored stain, which I re-paint each day, with my latest cup of coffee.

5:45 AM. Jesse awaits me. Her iris coating, her dusty windows, her bright lights, and her unique odor. She awaits me. I drive her down the monotone path, my eyes closed. I don't need to be reminded of the deep marks which her tires have implanted onto the road. No purpose for my looking for deer and fox for Jesse makes enough noise to wake the dead. While my ears dance continuously to the repetitive beat of her tires.

5:50 AM. Back at it again. Standing behind the disheartening wooden counter. Continuously tapping the desk bell, for that's how I entertain myself these days. And about now is when I start to think, and about now is when it all gets dangerous, hazardous… my thoughts lead to perilous endings…

5:55 AM. Something or rather someone's interrupts my thinking: out pops one of the two bulky entrance doors, as an extremely well-dressed group of six march into the room. Finally.

Something out of the ordinary. I rearrange my tie and pretend to be extremely absorbed in the 'dining rules' parchment, which I pick up in haste.

"Excuse me? Is this the reception?" The tallest of the group asks, her voice extremely polished, and moderate in tone. She gently scratches the top of her curly, caramel hair which rests professionally behind her bare ears.

"Is this the reception?" another asks even before I have time to respond.

"Well, what does it look like?" I hear myself say, moving my eyes back towards the neatly written words on the paper, which I still hold in my hands. My hands shake with excitement.

"That was rude," I hear another comment quietly, half-snickering, at my response. I had to look up to notice it was a man, for when he opened his mouth, a sharp-edged, squeaky noise filled the air, like the sound my granny's flip-flops would make when they were soaked from the rain.

"So may we check-in?" one of them implores, his voice is ever-so demanding.

"Check-in starts at 6:00," I tell him, keeping my eyes on the paper, nevertheless I can feel his aggravated gaze clouding my scalp.

"It's '57," he says, while a couple of them talk amongst themselves, in the back.

"Check-in starts at 6:00," I repeat. Thankfully he doesn't argue back, as I hear their footsteps fiercely stomp towards the lounging area over which my registration desk towers.

A few minutes later I hear their footsteps rewind.

"It's 6:00. Now let us check-in," he says, not even bothering to be polite. Not that he was really trying beforehand, anyway.

"Well, I suppose I could do that," I snap, placing down the document, which was still in my rigid hands. This time I look up at him, the guy I had been talking to, he seems as if he purchased his sandy blond hair from a men's magazine: extremely patted down and showered with bottles and bottles of gel. A small nose. Amber eyes. After what seems like minutes, he speaks again.

"Don't you want my name?" he questions, as I foretell a sigh will soon accompany his words, and I listen, as my prediction was correct.

"Okay then, tell me your name," I say, finally placing my fingertips on the dusty keys. Ah, how I've missed the diverse, elegant sound that each key makes.

"Carter. Samuel Carter," he sighs, projecting his voice a tad.

"Mhm, okay," I respond, as his eyes instruct me to say something more, however I don't obey his command.

"I'm in a room with-" he half-groans, as he sees I'm not paying any attention. He seems to be extremely annoyed at my behavior.

I type some more, as I discover a few more keys I notice how around half of the keys are now free from the carpeting dust.

"Sam, move aside," the squeaky guy shouts. He is a slim, rather tall guy. However, next to the guy beside him, he not only looks short, but also freakishly skinny. I maintain my poker face, while my thoughts do a bit of story-telling, for example: how many puffs of wind can blow this guy to the ground? Three? No two, two, I am practically certain.

"You listen here," he implores; his light eyes burn with impatience. "We are all very tired from our flight, so you either help us, quickly… or I will call the manager," he threatens me, and I look at him for a second, a little taken-aback, but after all, this attitude was expected.

"I am the manager. So you can either have some patience or leave," I shot back, trying my best to avoid the grin which wants to find its way across my ever-so pale face.

"Fine! I will leave," he says, a French accent highlights his words, echoing throughout the room. As he starts to take off, a stubby, lion-maned girl mumbles something to his elf-like ear and he puts his sack back down.

"One room consists of Smith. Scarlett Smith," Samuel continues, now pointing to the stubby, lion-maned girl, her eyes dark in color. "The other room is for myself, Pierre Andre', Griffin Paddock," he follows, pointing to the guy who previously tried to leave, and next to him, a rather bulky man. Dark of color, while his eyes portray a golden-hearted figure. He looks like an uplifting type of guy, but then again, first-impressions are well, only that, first-impressions. I move my eyes to the last of the bunch, a dark haired, burnt umber eyed, light-skinned, guy. His eyes portray some sense of excitement as well as desperation at the same time, but under it all his eyes are empty. He is a little bit chubby here and there, but very well dressed, from head to toe. "Allen Fredrick."

"Here are the two keys," I tell them, handing them two antique, Victorian-styled rusty keys across the counter.

"You might want to give the doors a good push before entering," I add, proud of myself that I have been helpful, and instead of 'thank you's' I receive hollow stares. What a strange generation.

"Yeah, okay. What are the room numbers?" requests Samuel. Now that I have taken a better look at the lad, his gaze is quite like the one of a big cat. More specifically, a cheetah's, very impatient as well as selfish, and extremely bipolar.

"Room twenty-three for the first room," I announce.

"And for us?" Samuel asks, restless. I must say, the more he talks, the more impatient he appears.

"It's…" I look at my computer. "Room number…thirteen."

"Just thirteen?" he asks, and thankfully I knew what he meant.

"Yes, when I first built the place, I found it extremely foolish to start the room numbers from 100, like every other hotel. Why not from 1, you know?" I explain, as I receive another wave of stares. Whatever, I'm not here to make friends.

"Would you like me to show you to the rooms?" I offer, in the gentlest voice, I'd ever heard my crusty lips project.

"No, thanks," Pierre responds coldly, or rather squeaks.

"Well suit yourselves," I coldly respond back. I will perfectly mirror his attitude, if I must.

"Your name, sir?" someone asks me, although I didn't quite catch who it was.

"Larry," I respond, pointing to the name tag, pinned at the left of my chest.

They mount up the stairs, snowed with a rose colored carpet. As soon as they pass I switch on the Persian blue stained glass chandelier and suddenly the whole place lights up, like it used to. What a beauty she is! She has awoken from her hibernation. She is up and running. I take a long sigh, and wait for it all to begin.

The walnut floor, enhancing a sense of warmth and safety. The tallest of ceilings, painted with detail after detail, until the white background stands no more. The waterfall carpet, carefully placed in the middle of the stair steps, revealing around a couple feet of wood on each side. As the spiral scroll railing accompanies the stairs up to every floor.

The day has sprinted by, my guests stayed in their rooms all day. Now, it's almost dinner, and I awaken her belly, the dining room. I await for my guests to arrive… And once again the minutes fly by. I remind myself that my precious time is like water in a vast tub, it circles the drain, till it slowly pours all out. The bottom of the bathtub turns dry.

I open the dynamic golden-framed doors and switch on the fierce lights. Wow! Never did I remember her like this. It's almost the same as it used to be, well aside from the spider webs which have dominated the place and the dust which has unfortunately decided to move in, without pre-notice. I can almost hear the music which played on the stage, music which played for the people, for their unfulfilling enjoyment and their maximum content. I can taste that divine nourishment that filled each and every one of their stomachs to the peak. I can see the smiles and wide-eyed faces of all the pretty people, each dressed in clothes and riches finest of all the lands. Mostly, I can still smell that bitter but vivid scent of champagne rushing and navigating in those colossal, transparent glasses, for which I purely crave for…

"Sir?" I see her, the caramel haired girl and her flushed face, as she enters the gallant, gold room. Now that I think about it, I forgot to register her down in the room with the lion-maned girl. What was her name?

"It's Renata. Renata Urbani," she acknowledges. Ah, yes, must have slipped my ancient mind.

"Yes," I say, grabbing a chair, and attempting to sit down. Suddenly, it breaks and I fall to the floor with a splat to my fragile body. I can merely see her, as she immediately sprints to where I have fallen on the floor. She helps me back up, or rather pulls me back up, and I hear her calling out to me, or at least I think it's me whose name is flying out of her mouth, and she's asking me so many darn questions and… and…

"Oh my! Thank goodness you're okay," she exclaims immediately as I open my eyes. This girl can't give me a break, huh?

"What in the world?" I shout, as her bare face is centimeters to mine "Can't you move your face a tad?"

"Yes, sorry. You just have a bump on your forehead, I wanted to see if you needed cream or a medicine of some sort," she explains in a rush, while vigorously tapping her phone a few times to the patterned carpet which mirrors the ceiling of the dining room.

"It's no use," I point out.

"What isn't?" she asks.

"That," I acknowledge pointing to her continuous motion. "Your phone. It's no use, there is no internet in this entire hotel. Ha! If only the whole land was free of the internet and electricity and all that weird technology you kids use today, we'd see more of 'em stars in the black sky. Hell, I guess no one would have a fat wallet in their pocket, either."

"There is no internet…" she seems concerned, I would be too, if I was accustomed to having the phone as my owner. "Well, okay, where is the closest town?"

"Whatever for?" I implore, offended that already she wants to leave when she has only just arrived. Or worse, her desperation for the internet when there is so much beauty here.

"For cream," she says. "For the lump, or rather, hill that is building up on your forehead."

"Oh, no worries. There has been more of these hills, vaster ones too," I explain, smiling, as she mirrors my expression.

"I'd still like to know, though, how far the closest town is. I'd like to talk to my dad sometimes," she adds, as her taupe eyes turn back to her useless phone.

"Erm, about five to six days of driving. Four if you're lucky, but never seen anyone do it in four." I tell her, as I receive a worried look, my answer is certainly not what she was looking for.

"Mmm," she groans disappointedly.

"I suppose your father will have to wait."

"I guess so…" she sighs, with a rather troubled face. More troubled than she should be.

Is everything all right? What is troubling you? Is what I wanted to ask, but I learned better than to meddle into other's business. Meddling only hurts the sensitive soul, even if helping may be a kind act. Still, I wonder what's pinching her on the inside.

"I should go now and organize my clothes. Are you sure you don't need anything?"

"Yes, now go on, I have food to cook," I respond, surprised at how generous she is. What's she doing hanging around with the rest of those knuckle-heads?

"Okay then. When's dinner?"

"At 8:30, as it's always been."

She smiles and saunters out the door, as the last words emerge from my mouth. I hastily make my way to the kitchen, which hasn't been in use for ages. Just as I enter I remember just how many years have passed since I've cooked a meal, a real meal, and just too many, too many years, way too many. Regardless, I can still, scarcely, remember her amiable smile, which always reminded me of an up-side- down rainbow, lively and vivid. I remember teaching her, her very first meal: buttered-chicken, which included a side of roasted potatoes and a jam sauce on top. Her wide, eager eyes made my day every single time. She had such an ambition to do it all.

I still am able to find the pan rack ceiling which I had constructed myself a while back. I remember, still holding the heavy hammer in my once-soft, smooth hand. However, I look down, many of the pans have fallen from the rack onto the floor, which isn't in great shape either. Many tiles are broken, or chipped and have moved from their original placing. I still admire the jet black, iron oven, which my mother had gifted me, or rather the hotel, on the hotel's twentieth anniversary. Or better known as, the second opening of the hotel. I think back to the opening day of the hotel, she was so proud of me, so insanely proud. I think back to when her reassuring hand rested on my shoulder, while I cut the red ribbon, announcing the second, official opening of the hotel. Cheers and champagne had accompanied my words.

I scan over the dead herbs which have rotted in their cream-colored ceramic pots, along with the once delicious, flavored smell. I used to have the best conversations with my herbs, especially Josephine. Although, I must say Cecilia, did make me laugh the most.

Yes, I haven't got the best remarks when I inform listeners that I talk to my plants, regardless I don't care.

However, my apron is what grasps my mind back to the past: I touch the apron, my apron, which is hung over the chair, her chair. It remains there, just where I left it…

The very one which she would beg to borrow from such a young age. I'd tell her no. And yet, it was only the once, only that single time, I told her 'no'… to this very day.

Barely seconds pass before a shrieking noise wanders its way through rooms and rooms, all the way to my old-aged but, still lively, ears. I ambled my way up the stairs, slowly and steadily, like a sly fox. Passing by all the paintings and banners which adorn her walls. I reach the second floor, and I hear some of my guests talking rapidly, while others quietly and others again, anxiously.

"Say something. Say something! I'm begging you." I hear a familiar shout, Renata's I'd say.

"How did this happen, Griffin?" This time it's Samuel, his voice stern, and severe. Nonetheless, the shock manages to highlight his every word.

"I- I don't know," whispers a voice, which I can't connect to its owner. Most likely Griffin's.

"Griffin, you were in the room, while the rest of us were out. What's happened?" Samuel implored once more. At this, I can practically feel the floor shake, as my ears ring.

"I- I was taking a shower. I wasn't in the darn bedroom!" he utters, practically forgetting how one is supposed to speak. His fright is audible. "I had music on. I did, I swear. It wasn't me!"

Thankfully, I find a decent spot to observe the situation without any of them realizing of my looking and of my listening.

"You sure seem defensive." Samuel roars, while he clenches his cleanly shaved jaw. "I hadn't even accused you. I just asked you a simple question."

"Maybe… maybe we should accuse you?" Samuel adds; his breathing, uncontrolled and chaotic. Renata touches Samuel's forearm and looks at him in those furious eyes. Unfortunately, from the angle I'm at, I cannot tell what Griffin's eyes are displaying, I'm guessing fright, from his tone of voice.

"Shush one second, will you, please? We need everyone here, this is-" Renata starts saying, with this calm shielded voice, but under that shield, she's the most frightened of them all. "Terrible."

I finally get a glance at Renata's face and I find myself staring, in utter disbelief. Her face has turned two or three shades paler. Her once rosy cheeks have melted, revealing fresh snow. Her hand twitches by her side, as she continuously swallows that unbearable pit in the middle of her throat.

"What do we do?" Griffin murmurs to himself, more than to the others. It's only now that I see the blood trickling down his guilty hands.

"Where is Pierre?" Samuel screams, and just as he does, Pierre and lion-maned girl come from around the corner of the hallway.

"Here is he," he squeaks joyfully, while his left hand is entwined to the lion-maned girl's right.

"You guys really can't stay away from me for too long can you?" he adds, smirking, while lifting his eyebrow. Who does he think he is? The king of the jungle? Or rather the king of them knuckle-heads. Anyway, Samuel doesn't seem to be too happy with him either.

"Shut up, and look at what's happened!" Samuel instructs, annoyed to the very max. Renata doesn't speak a word, she's gone mute. He then points his

long finger inside the room, room thirteen, the guys'
room. As his eyes and lion-haired girl 's move in the
direction of Samuel's finger. They stare attentively.

"Allen is dead." Pierre quavers.

Chapter two

My vivid vision maneuvers its way, following the indication of Samuel's finger, into the room.

My eyes rest on Allen's lifeless body, which lies on the carpet floor. I stare at his face, which has turned to a sap green tint, his dark eyes with no soul, hollow as ever and rolled to the back of his head, his slim, innocent, statue-like lips parted, revealing a slither of front tooth. His hair is in chaos and I can't help but admire the fact that it looks torn and pulled. My glance moves lower onto his broad body, his flannel unbuttoned all the way, revealing a dark stain on his undershirt, under his ribcage, towards the right. Just as I try to take a glance at the rest of them, Samuel closes the door, blocking my view of the situation.

Ugh. I need to figure out what happens, what they will do next. I must figure out a plan, but it is rather late and I would much rather go to sleep at the moment. Then again, it haunts me to sleep, it's all rather frightening. There has never been a murder at the hotel.

I advance up the stairs, one heavy foot after the other, to the very last floor, to a room at the peak of the hotel. I sometimes sleep there when guests are here. I grab my key, from inside my deep, pant pocket and place the key in the keyhole. I step inside and I'm immediately grateful that I had previously cleaned it out for it had been in worse condition than the kitchen and the dining room combined. I strip off my clothes, and take a cold shower. Every day I manage to turn the knob a little more to the colder side. My cold tolerance seems to be increasing, well, that is expected. I exit the bathroom, and slip on my silk bed robes, I climb into bed, just after having set my alarm for 5 am. I turn my body to face the four-paneled window, embraced by a smooth, wooden frame. The wood, the color my mother had on her head: mocha brown. My eyelids close themselves and I wish I could dream but I unwillingly enter a pitch black bubble.

After what feels like a few minutes I am awoken by a call. I sit up and check the clock, it's 3 am, that would explain my need to use the bathroom. I grab a candle, bring it to life, and move it closer to the window, where the call came from. Griffin! Griffin! Griffin! It calls, over and over, and then it stops, just like that. Strange.

My alarm shrieks two hours later, and after having been awoken at three, I haven't heard any more of them calling him and I am a light sleeper so, if there had been more calls, I would have heard them for sure. I'm assuming that it had been Samuel calling out to Griffin last night, because it sounded like a deep voice which very closely resembled Samuel's. But at three in the morning? Does nobody have any manners? Couldn't he wait till a tad later in the morning? I really wish I knew what was so important.

At eight o'clock I await my guests in the dining room. Only five minutes later, they show up.

"Good morning!" I greet them with a grin.

"Hello," a rather dry response from Samuel.

"Where is erm… Weren't you a party of six?" I ask, knowing I need to put up an act, because for all they know, I have no clue of what happened last night.

"Oh um yes…" Samuel says, as the lion-maned girl shivers, and her iguana eyes fog up with tears. As we make eye contact she hides her face in Pierre's arms. I can already tell that these five aren't good at hiding secrets.

"Allen's not hungry," Samuel finally spits, throwing a nasty look at the lion-maned girl.

I don't respond.

They barely touch their share of meal, which consists of a wide plate filled to the max with, still-sizzling bacon, warm butter spread on soft, hearty bread, runny eggs, and roasted potatoes, which create a delicious aroma in the air.

After their breakfast, I informed them of a special privilege we have at the hotel, "As you are my guests, it is my duty and responsibility that housekeeping will be done in the rooms in which you are temporarily staying." They all looked at each other in shock, probably because poor Allen was still lying on the hotel floor.

"Oh no, it's rather alright, we can manage on our own," Samuel spoke, as rapidly as ever.

"Oh but I must." I implore. I never implore. But this time, my mind has wrapped itself around a rather peculiar idea from the depths of my sleep.

"No, no-" Renata continues, as Samuel interrupts her.

"We don't trust maids!" he blurs out, while a faint tint of red appears on his slim-framed face.

"Oh, but Thalia is excellent. Never sinned once in her entire life, I promise you," I reassure them.

"We just don't..." Samuel raises his voice a tad.

I cut him off. "It isn't a choice, it's a privilege and you, my friend, will take it. Be grateful some more, won't you?"

"Okay thank you, we just need to grab some belongings first," Pierre says in a rush.

"Well, alright, I suppose I could tell Thalia to clean the room after breakfast," I say, holding back a manipulative, crooked grin.

"I really appreciate it, sir," Renata replies.

"You can all visit the indoor pool, if you long for a swim," I inform them, as I pick up the plates.

"Thank you," she says, getting up from her seat. "Scarlett, won't you come with me?"

I have learned two things in this short conversation, number one, they have no idea how to mask a secret, or rather a body and secondly, I'm reminded that the lion-mane's name is Scarlet.

After they all finish breakfast they head to the pool and my plan begins. I go to the last floor of the hotel, the fifth floor, and tap a tiny button on the ceiling. A tile protrudes, and a ladder pops out. After having climbed the ladder, I find myself inside the attic, which is by far the worst affected by the aging of the times. I skip over the chaos and open the golden-framed chest, adorned with rubies at the sides, placed against a peeling wall right where I had left it in: the farthest corner of the attic. Inside I find her maid uniform, her diaries, her belongings, and her picture frame. Her soul.

"I know I've promised to never touch your possessions, but it's an emergency, my dear," I whisper to her, while admiring the black and white photograph. In this picture, she looks young, in her mid-thirties if I'm not wrong. Although I've seen this particular picture so many times, each time I see it I remain breathless, dumb shook even. Her projecting jaw dominates her face, and grabs your eyes in a matter of seconds. Her narrow, wolf eyes, stroke my delicate heart. Her pearl necklace, which covers parts of her broad collarbones, and her long neck. While her slim lips, which speak no more.

I take the uniform and whisper "RIP, Thalia, I love you, my dearest." I kiss the photograph, and place it back inside the chest. I take a few more items, required in order for my plan to be a success, and leave the attic. Next, I enter the bathroom.

Chapter three

I remove my Prussian blue button-down, my ironed pants. I slip Thalia's uniform over my pale skin. As I had expected it is extremely tight and snug. How did she survive in this uniform? Well, she had a slim body frame, I can still remember her silhouetted figure dancing in front of the moonlight. I reach for some color, and tap it onto my face. All the times in which I have seen Thalia do this, it had never once occurred to me that it is very difficult to get the perfect consistency right. I find myself a blond wig (although Thalia had long, strong, dark, chestnut hair), and place it over my remaining- gray hairs. I slip a pair of trick glasses over the bridge of my nose. After completing this, I find my equipment which is required to 'clean' the rooms. As I arrive at the first room, room number 13, as I had predicted, Renata awaits me.

"Hello you must be Thalia?" she looks at me. Have I disguised myself enough? Can she tell it's me? If she figures me out, not only will my plan fail, but it will remove all the remaining slithers of trust which she has placed into this hotel.

"Y-yes," I say, in the highest pitched voice I can make. "Sorry, I am not allowed to talk to the guests." I stutter, trying to find my way out of having conversation, because that never turns out well.

"Oh, sorry. I just wanted you to know that there is a faint stain on the floor, it's fruit punch," she explains smiling, as I look at her. She's telling me that Allen's blood stain is fruit punch? Oh? Oh, lord help them.

"Yes ma'am," I respond, thank goodness she finally decides to step aside.

I take my cleaning cart inside the room, and quickly redo the beds so that it looks as if I had done my duty. Or rather, Thalia had. After having placed a new soap bar into the shower slot, I decide to examine the stain on the floor. Poor kid.

Not only will this stain be permanently marked into the carpet of this room, but tattooed into this hotel's history. Of one thing I am most certain, nobody can ever know of this. Nobody.

I have finished my maid's duty, but the best part is yet to come. I must look for the dagger, or knife, which stabbed the living soul out of a body. I check everywhere possible but nothing. Failing in doing so, the second part of my plan comes into play. I place a listening device, a bug, on the top of the window sill and cover it with the translucent flower-themed curtain.

After having done so, in both room thirteen and room twenty-three, I head back to room thirteen, to grab my original clothes, which I temporarily kept under the queen bed.

As I reach down for my clothes, I accidentally grasp something different. I pull out my hand, as I observe the folded piece of lined paper. I open it, as I begin to read in a whisper.

"Allen,

I'm so sorry. I wish it hadn't happened. But it had to happen. I had to. I had to push you out. I wanted to forget you. I needed to forget you. Because you ruined me.

But the truth is... that it wasn't your fault. Or maybe it was.

You always admired all your success, all your passions, your goals. You made me remember I had none. Which is exactly why, my family was more proud of you than they have ever been of me. As you story-told with starry eyes.

You only needed me when you had to cope. Or blamed me because of your coping. I can't handle it anymore. I can't. And I'm sorry. I'm weak.

So, it's not true, all the lies I told you. One being that I have to leave. I don't have to leave for Asia next year with my family. I made it up. But for now, it's better you think that way.

Griffin."

I flip the letter over.

"And why am I writing these, if I won't send them?"

I stuff the letter back to its original place, and leave.

The sun has taken his comfort upon the glossy pond which greets the entrance of my hotel. Hotel Everly. My grandma's hotel.

"Please tell me! Please grandma!" I beg of her, in the depths of night. It's the fourth night in a row, in which I'm scared of the monster under my bed.

"Alright, alright," she sighs, with a sensitive smile. "Well, my dear grandson, as you know, I never did like my given name, Katherine. It was my mother's name as well, and my mother and I had a-too many differences, you could say. Every chance I got, I would change my name. Ophelia was what I changed it to, while I was at war…"

"War, isn't that where you met him?" I ask, knowing she would never reveal the slightest hint of who my grandfather was.

"Larry! We don't talk about that bastard," she squirms. My grandma, one of the most patient and forgiving women alive on this planet, I think, and the moment I mention him, she gets furious. So insanely unforgiving. "Do you want to hear my story or not?"

"Yes, sorry grandma," I apologize, as her eyes lowered their weapons, they turn back into her bitter-sweet amber eyes.

"Well, during the war, Everly was the purple team's leader-"

"The enemy? Grandma! You named your grand hotel after the enemy leader? Grandma, how could you?" I begged curiously, infuriated too. I had never heard this little detail.

"Now, son, let me finish. On the eighty-ninth day of the war, at 5:15 pm, I raised my white flag as a sign of…"

"Surrender!" I shout, gaping at her.

"No, not surrender. As a sign of… as a sign of collaboration, as seconds later Everly does the same. For ages later people have admired me, and worshipped me for they told me I was such an *inspiration to them all, for finding peace in the darkest hours. For being the bigger person, some may say.*

"Well, that wasn't exactly the truth. You see, that same day, while the newly sun shined its dense rays upon his land, for the first time that day, she snuck up on me. She caught me while I was alone. Disarmed me to the skin, and covered my mouth with a filthy handkerchief. For all I knew, she was the enemy. I thought that was the end of me. I remember kicking her, with all my might while the taste of sweat and dirt flushed out into my mouth from the handkerchief. As I attempted to run away, she tied me to a tree. She tied my wrists together and lifted my arms up and over the knife placed inches above my head. I just stared at my bow and my multiple arrows which laid, scattered on the ground, useless as ever. She then tied my ankles together tightly, with knots so extremely complex. I thought I was breathing my last breaths, and taking my last look at this world. Luckily, she had come in peace."

"Thank goodness grandma," I say, as she chuckled. "After you finish the story, can I have a glass of milk?"

She nods. "I can get it for you now, if you like."

"No! Finish the story," I beg.

"Okay, okay. It's not a story though, it happened, Larry. To me," she explains.

"Oh, I know, grandma," I tell her, as she places my bed covers over my shivering shoulders.

"Well Everly told me to do as she said, and initially I was going to disregard everything she was

going to tell me, as long as I came out of it alive. She told me to raise the white flag..."

"So, to surrender, grandma. Like I said?" I ask.

"Well, that's what I thought as well. So I looked at her, thinking how could she possibly think I'd do anything that comes from her mouth. She told me that at 5:15 pm, I had to do it, and seconds later she would do the same. She wanted us all to have the land, to share it, for eternity. I then asked her why was I the one who had to put my flag up first, and she said 'Well, so your community, your people, your family, will think of you as a hero. Who saved them all.' Then she let me go, just like that. All day, I thought and thought about her words. Ringing in my ears. I recalled her eyes, and I kept remembering looking into them, and for some particular reason, wishing I had found them guilty.

At the end of the day, I was fatigued. Worn out, to the toe. I was going to do as she had said, because after all, she hadn't killed me. And she certainly had the chance.

At 5:15 pm, I raised my white flag, as it flapped in the wind, seconds later hers did the same. We initially shook hands, indicating the beginning of our friendship. And then patted one another on the back, we weren't formal, hell, we'd been at war! Our people allied and met one another, while others began to head home. Everly was such a mature person and one day, or in another life, I wish I can be half as much of saint as her," she terminated her words with tears to her eyes.

"Why are you crying, grandma?" I ask her. "Are you sick?"

"Oh, no, son. I'm happy," she explains, grinning, as she gets up to go grab me a glass of milk.

The sun has now begun to dive into the lake, while her rays like snakes, slither their way through millions of trees, blinding the eternal glaring eyes of audience. I rest my finger upon the frigid glass, as my breathing condenses the window. And I do, as I used to do, when I was little, I inscribe a heart in it, and color it in.

<u>Chapter four</u>

After dinner, I decide I want to enlighten my guests with a special, traditional evening dance. I tell them all to meet me in the ballroom at 10:30.

10:30 pm had arrived in the blink of an eye, and nobody was to be seen. I wait by the entrance doors in my suit, which took me several hours to find, and long minutes to iron. I hoped to see them soon, but, the feeling in the back of my mind knows they won't come. After my personal horrid experiences, I always expect the worst possible outcome, because nothing is worse than THE worse.

10:50 pm, nobody. Not even a shadow, hiding about.

10:55, all my excitement has officially exited my antiquated body.

11:05 pm, I see Renata running towards me.

"Larry, sir!" She calls out, running up the staircase.

I raise my hand, in objection. I don't want to hear any excuses, of any sort.

"I'm so, so sorry we are late, Pierre thought we had to come at 11pm, and then I remembered it was actually 10:30 pm, and..."

"It's okay, really," I lie, as I tighten my tie. I guess I can accept this excuse, just this once.

"Thank you for waiting," she responds, as her dangling, silver earrings sparkle under the warm candle lights. Her puffy hair cascades over her rich, dark lavender dress.

"Here come the others," I point out, more to myself. I watch as a kaleidoscope of sparkles and shimmers approaches the door. "Let us begin!"

I open the ballroom doors. My heart definitely takes a somersault in my chest. My excitement is over the top, higher than the moon.

The ballroom, her sweet place. The hotel's fun side, her social, amusing, enthusiastic side. Anyone who steps inside is certain to recall this moment for the rest of their lives.

I channel my inner joy and lead my guests inside. As soon as we enter, a wave of gasps leave their mouths. I can't help but appreciate the golden, floral designs painted by hand on the white walls. The warmth and playful feeling coming from the lights, which enhance the place, from the floor to the high ceiling. The windows enrich the feeling of protection, as an emptiness camouflages itself outside. My feet slide as I glide across the room.

Just as I place a disk into the phonograph, my mind let's itself slip away for a while...

"Just wear the white dress Thalia!" I plead, desperately, hearing the guests flood inside the ballroom.

"No! White represents innocence." she cries.

"So?" I complain, I couldn't understand what the big deal was. The preacher can't stall any longer.

"But I'm not innocent, Larry!" she explains. "I killed hundreds, fighting. I can't ever forget that. And, no I'm not ashamed of it."

So she wore blue.

As I await at the bow of the room, the grand piano playing, soft, gentle music. I admire the room, decorated with flowers of all the kinds, ravishing red, party pink, brilliant blue. While golden framed chairs are placed row after row. Two hundred thirty-seven rows of chairs, to be exact. A slim, refined carpet in the middle of the rows, which she will soon walk upon.

"Here comes the bride... Here comes the bri-" a little boy calls out, as his mother claps his mouth, and scolds him.

There she is, in dark blue, as the end of her dress trails behind her, concealing her feet. Diamonds shower her hair, while a sword sits in her hands. Wait what?

"Is that a sword?" I hear myself shout. Oh no. I've always hated being the center of attention. Now everyone turns their glare at me. Why do they keep staring at me? She's the one with a massive sword in her hands.

I watch as people start to stand, scared that one of them will be the victim of a murder. It isn't rare to witness a wedding turn into a war zone. Thankfully, this isn't the case, I hope. I pray.

"Where is everyone going?" Thalia shouts, as she stops frozen. "Stay calm! Please."

I hear people murmur, nobody moves, out of fright. But nobody remains seated either.

"This is a tradition. Larry's grandmother brought a sword to her wedding too." she shouts and just at that moment I realize what a fool I have been. I bang my hand on my forehead, and inhale deeply.

"Thalia! Drop the sword." I roar, aggressively, as I make my way down to her.

"What are you doing? You said…" Thalia holds the sword closer to her body.

"Thalia. Hand me the sword," I am now inches from her face and I can see the diamonds circling her confused eyes. "Please."

She does as I say, and I take her soft hand to the makeshift altar. The music thankfully starts replaying and the guests take their seats once again.

While the priest talks, I zone out. I have made such a terrible mistake. An awful mistake. I start to think. Overthink. Who are these people? Who is this priest? Is he even a priest, or does he just pretend to be so? Why can't I be a priest? I'm going out of my mind.

"…gathered by love and-"

"Stop, stop, stop!" I pant. I fall down to my knees and cry. I cry like a punished baby.

"What's wrong?" Thalia whispers in my ear as she takes my hand and slowly moves her thumb up and down over my knuckles. I look at her, through this layer of despair depicted by tears. She understands.

"Um… can everyone listen up please?" she shouts, as barely one person listens.

"Everyone leave! Now!" she picks up the sword, by my feet. As soon as everyone sees the sword in her hand, they get frightened, of course they do. They scatter out the room like mice. Even the musician left his piano sheets, and scarpered. The priest left his bible, and exited the room.

"Thank you," I gasp, as she hugs me.

I grab the ring which was dropped by the ring bearer whom we trusted immensely. I picked it from

the ground, and placed it on Thalia's long, slim,
calloused finger. She does the same.

"I'm sorry I ruined the wedding, I -" I apologize.

"I never wanted this. I never wanted any of this,"
she stands indicating the room, the flowers, the
lights. "I just wanted you."

I grab two wine glasses, and fill them a little
above the half mark.

"I should say sorry," I sigh, as I indicate the
sword.

"Explain," she implores.

"I'm sorry you made a fool of yourself."

"Explain," she insists.

"Well, my grandmother, she did the same. She
brought a sword, or rather dagger, to her wedding,
the sword which allied her people with her enemies.
A token of gratitude, of peace..." I can't stand to
look her in the eyes.

"The dagger which my grandmother took to her
wedding was this big," I hold my hands 30 cm from
each other. Her eyes widen and she laughs. I look at
her amused.

"I-I carried a 95 cm sword to our wedding," she
says in between laughs.

"Yes, dear. You are one of a kind," I smile.
"That's not all..." My face falls.

"My grandma split with him, even before I met
him," I explain.

"Your grandfather?" she questions.

"He's not my grandfather. I-I don't know who he
is, and I don't want to know. He left my
grandmother in her most difficult time," I say, trying
to keep my calm.

"How could you not tell me? I'm sorry, I'm sorry about it all," sincerely she gushes, as she drops the wine glass, the red color invading the fabric of the dress.

"Let's go to sleep," I stand, as I take her right hand.

"You see I'm glad I wore blue," she smirks. *"Easier to remove the wine stain."*

"Larry! Larry." Renata shouts. "Finally!"

"Sorry, what's wrong?" I say, blinking a couple times. Where did everyone else go? Why is she the only one left?

"I found this on the ground, do I throw it out?" Renata asks me, as she hands me a patch of silk blue cloth. I smile, and take it from her. I look around the room, once more. Where is everyone?

"Also, it's 3 am, you should…"

"It's what?"

"It's 3 am, you should go home," she clarifies.

"Yes, I…" I run out of the room. Then I stop. I slowly breathe in and out. And afterwards, resume my sprint.

I run out the room, out of the front door, out into the woods, to my car. I get inside and cry. I collapse like a bird with no wings. My heart crumbles like ashes from a previous fire. My hands shake on the steering wheel.

One hour later, I pick myself up, place my mind back onto my shoulders. I start the car and head back to the cabin, to home. In less than two hours I must be back at the hotel. Ah, there is the cabin. I can't wait to have a good night's sleep. I'm about to park by the side of my cabin and I can't stop.

I press my foot harder onto the brake. I put more and more force on the pedal until my leg shakes. CRANK! I break the pedal off. I have passed my cabin by meters now. Trees and more trees run by. Accelerating by the second. I'm headed towards a steep cliff, I've completely lost control. I try to jump out of the car, but the doors are shut tight, and won't budge. The windows, blocked. The car sprints uphill, I see the tip of the cliff getting closer and closer. There are no more trees, they have all vanished, only a forlorn road. The tip of the cliff is so near. Please no. No! No!

"Help, Help!" I hear myself mumble.

The car flies off the cliff, I'm heading for the ocean. I bang on the window of the car, it's no use, I've never been physically strong. I scream, but for what? Even if anyone could hear me, who would save me? The aggressive waves attack the car as soon as it falls into the water. The water starts to fill the car in seconds. I feel my socks getting wet. The water torments all the way to my thighs. My fingertips touch the frigid water, so thin, so vulnerable. I look out at the horizon, the sun emerges from the water, leaving an orange, pink, tint into the sky, like a watercolor painting. I smile, look at the sun, and close my eyes as my head falls on the wheel, making the car horn's honk, continuous and repetitive, no stops in between.

I've heard all sorts of greatest fears, suicide, insects, crowded spaces, the dark, abandonment, heights, drowning, not succeeding, uselessness. But mine - mine is loneliness. And dying, one's greatest fear, is the worst fear of all.

<u>Chapter five</u>

I can still feel the spinning. The sharp stinging sensation in my nose, in my mouth, choking harder and harder, like what sadness does to one after time. The worst part is that sadness does it slowly, and painfully. Making you question it all.

My heavy heart floats to the surface for the first time, except I'm still dying. Dead, maybe. How will I know when I'm dead? Thalia. What if I forget about her? My grandma? Stop thinking for once. Feel the extravagance of emptiness and soak it up.

I feel myself cough, again and again, and again, and again. And finally, I open my eyes. I see a soft, light blue sky. Am I in heaven? Surely hell isn't like this? I look around, and

I see the trees, I see the ground, I see the cliff, I am on the cliff.

I am alive. I must be. I pinch myself, to be certain. Ouch! Yes, my nerves still work. I slowly get up, and I see Renata shuffle from behind a tree.

"Larry, sir! You are alive!" she cries.

"How- what?" I'm puzzled.

"How did you get yourself into that situation? You have to be more careful," she warns me.

"Sorry," I hear myself say. Why am I apologizing? I'm petrified. I can't get a hold of what's going on.

"I had to save you," she scolds me. Why is she mad?

"You did?" I question.

"Yes! I almost died myself. A thank you would be enough."

"Thank you." I mutter.

"Now get up, it's already 2 pm!" she shouts, as she points to the shimmering watch on her wrist. "Sorry, you just gave me quite the scare. Never seen anyone this close to dying, you know?"

I nod, and stroll beside her back to my cabin. Getting up, was a journey itself, for my chest aches and my abdominal feels as though someone blew a balloon inside of it. How did Jesse's brakes fail me? I check them every other day, to soothe my paranoia, nevertheless, that wasn't enough. Once we reach my cabin, my breath seems to have left once again. Nonetheless, I give Renata a reassuring wave of the hand and she leaves and heads back to the hotel. I take a moment to help myself. To save myself.

Just as I allow my mind to doze off, to figure it all out on its own, I hear muffled voices from my headphones attached to the speakerphone. I run to listen.

"How could you not tell us?" Griffin demands.

"I didn't want to," Scarlet whispers.

"Well why not?" Samuel persist, banging his fist on a wall, or maybe a table.

"What's going on?" I hear Renata say. She's probably just arrived.

"Scarlet's bandana, around her neck, has been Allen's all this time," Samuel yells, more to himself.

"Allen's bandana?" Samuel whimpers.

"Since when did you have this?" Pierre implores, as I hear him tug it.

"Since he died," she says slowly, as her voice breaks.

"You mean you grabbed it while he was dead?" Samuel roars, as I hear his footsteps (heavy and strong) stomp on the floor. Does this mean she'd discovered Allen's body- dead, even before Griffin had?

"Scarlet- I don't even know what to say," Pierre sighs. "Samuel! Stop walking in circles."

"I felt bad that we ended on the wrong foot," Scarlet begins explaining.

"Oh, Scarlet," Pierre squeaks.

"Let me finish," Scarlet declares. "I wanted to remember him by something."

"Was the memory of him not enough?" Pierre cries.

"No!" Scarlet screams. "What's the matter with you guys anyway? I haven't committed a crime."

"The bandana was on his neck that night..." Renata states.

"Scarlet, you might have committed a crime," Griffin declares.

"That's true. The bandana was on his neck that night," Pierre follows up, stuck in-between his thoughts.

"You could have used the bandana, so there would be no fingerprints on the knife. Then you had this cover up story, as to why you stole the bandana," Samuel says, in a low voice.

Ah, so the weapon used to end Allen's miserable life was a knife. I scribble it down onto my hand. But just as I try, my eyes decide to swim and now

I'm seeing ten pens, on my ten hands. My head feels awfully dizzy. Unsteady.

"I want to go home," Scarlet shouts. "I'm so done with this. All of it!"

"Our driver can't come earlier, plus I can't move our flights," Griffin explains. "I want to leave this place too, trust me."

"Plus, we can't leave. What will we say about Allen? 'Oh hey, yes Mrs. Brown, he's dead,'" Renata whimpers.

"How can you guys let this go?" Samuel asks, his voice shaky. "She killed Allen."

"I have to agree with Samuel on this one, there is good evidence," Renata agrees.

"And, a motive," Samuel continues. "You didn't want Pierre to find out. For all we know, you could've had an affair."

"How dare you say such thing," Scarlet cries.

"Griffin, how could you let this go?" Samuel roars. "He was your best friend, and now it's all over. All…"

"Shut up!" Pierre and Griffin respond in sync.

"All of you! This place gives me the creeps," Pier squirms. His vulnerability, his terror is extremely evident in his voice.

I decide to take the headphones off; I've had enough of this. I'm heading over to the hotel. I sprint outside- oh right… no Jesse.

Once I've made my way to the hotel, by foot, it's around 5 pm, and I decide that it's better if they get a chance to relax.

"Excuse me," I project my voice, as they immediately stop talking and glance at me. "I was wondering if you all are interested in visiting the library?"

"Yes," Samuel responds immediately. Never took him as the book type.

"We may find some evidence as to how this all happened or something," he adds, almost silently. I heard him anyway, while I see Pierre jab him in the guts, and place his index finger over his lips.

I instruct them to follow me. They follow me to the second floor and down hallway. We are greeted by a revealing, extroverted window, at the very end of the hallway. We take the door to the right of the window and enter inside the library. A humble, modest area, with shelves filled with books and more books, from the carpet floor all the way to the smooth, monotone ceiling. Armchairs and couches complement the space, while a fireplace lies asleep. My grandma never wanted a fireplace in the library, if a fire started, it'd be the end of the hotel. But I convinced her. Therefore, it is my duty to keep the fire asleep until I feel safe leaving a bunch of kids in the room with fire.

I decide to remain in the library with them, for the simple fact that I yearn to read. It's been ages since I've lifted any type of manuscript.

I watch as they each pick out several books and manuscripts and begin reading, as I look for something to read as well.

After long minutes of decision, I find a diary with a grainy leather cover; I open it and find handwritten pages, filled to the rim with words, no margin blank. This is someone's diary. I feel a sort of thrill approaching my veins. I look around the room, and decide to take my reading to the outside.

"I will be outside, just let me know when you guys need anything," I say, as they nod in response.

I grab my coat from the coat rack and exit the hotel. I sit myself on the ground, with my curved back supported on a tree's trunk. I take out once again the diary from my coat's inner right pocket and I open it to a random page, just after the half-way mark. I shut my mind of all thoughts in order to focus on the reading.

I don't want to read words. I want to read moments.

Dearest Diary,

After decades and decades of relaxation and tranquility in the abide and control of our alliance, today it has all come crashing down upon us, like an Avalanche, only I wish it were an avalanche rather than hours and hours of bombing.

Here I was, sipping my coffee, in the comfort of the hotel's walls when I heard screams and shouts. Melancholy they were. I raced to see what it was, and flames had started devouring the hotel's ceilings. I was so extremely confused, for I had no clue as to what was occurring. I hastily ran outside the hotel, and saw aircrafts, and jets surrounding the hotel like wasps to honey. I took a closer look, and to my most bizarre surprise a bold, bright purple stripe was painted on the sides. The purple team had decided to ambush us!

I sprinted back inside, while more bombs fell from the smoky sky. The whole top floor was eaten away by the fierce and vicious flames. Furniture and lounging areas burned to the ground. Guests had been injured, if not killed.

I immediately told everyone to evacuate the building as I ran room to room, making sure that nobody was left behind.

I first found Odette, a pregnant lady, in her mid-twenties, lying desperately on the floor. Thankfully the flames hadn't gotten to her yet. I helped her up and carried her outside. On the way, I found Victor, the fire had started to demolish him. His clothes were on fire, which struck him to the boiling ground. His loyal eyes closed and his brave lips crisped. Goodbye, my brother…

Afterwards, hurdling each and every one of my emotions, my feelings, I go to check on my love, I found you screaming so loudly, a prominent vein in your neck looking as though it will pop. I'm only meters away from you, but a giant wooden beam surrounded by flames separates us. If you don't come to where I am, you will die. I have already lost my son, I cannot lose any more. I jump over the beam, as the fire spreads to the floor, to the walls, till we are surrounded completely by fire. The fire finds its way to my lungs, making me cough repeatedly. I shout at you, as an indication to cover your mouth with your shirt to avoid the toxic smoke. You do as I tell you.

I thankfully arrive to you and show you the way
out, just as I do, another beam falls, trapping me in
your previous corner. Now it is I who is trapped,
trapped by smoke and flames.

I have no more sight of you, but your voice is still
strong. Your voice yells louder than the sizzling
monster eating away at the wood, under my feet.

"Arthur!" you cry, as you noticed I am not right
behind you anymore.

"Go! Go!" I coughed. "You will die too if you
stay!"

"No!" you shrieked. "I'm not leaving you!" you
shout back, your voice shaky as ever.

"Do as I say!" I choke back, I inhale more and
more smoke. Will the smoke choke me to death? As
if I am a sinner at the hanging noose around my neck,
till I am suspended in midair. I'll be flying. Flying
dead.

"No! I will get you help!" you declare.

"I beg you, leave!" I shout again, as fire starts
crawling up my body. Or rather, will the fire eat me
alive? Like when a snake swallows his entire prey,
whole.

"Arthur?" you shout again. I need you to leave!
Otherwise, you will have the same fate, the same
destiny, as I.

"Leave!" I plead. "Leave!"

"I love you!" you wail.

I think of a happy place, I think of you, to avoid the pain building up on the outside and inside of my fighting body.

However, I make it out alive, or else how could I be telling you all this?

Lots of love, my dear,

Arthur

There are no words. No words. None, whatsoever. All the secrets that lie in the core of the hotel's walls are here, in this very diary. In my hands. Power. Knowledge.

All my questions about the hotel will be soon answered… I hope.

From just one small entry I have been injected with such immense comprehension: I have been informed as to why Hotel Everly had been closed for so many years: enemy bombing. The re-building must have taken ages! Secondly, if grandma said that she named the hotel after the purple team's leader, does that mean Everly betrayed her? Or did the purple team have a different leader by then? Questions, and the yearning for answers entwine around my brain, till I find myself in a vast space of absence. Longing to know my own story. Which is mine, by all means to behold. It is my past. It is my family who ran the hotel, the least they could do was tell me what tormented the hotel for so many years. However, what I'm most confused about, is: who is Arthur?

I carefully close the diary, and head back to my guests.

Right as I am about to enter the room, I hear them reading something aloud. What have they found? Is it another diary? What if these- these strangers learn about my background, my past, the hotel's past, even before I do. I place my ear to the door:

"This next one is called Foul Liberty" Griffin informs the rest.

"Okay, read it to us," Scarlet responds.

Chapter six

"It goes like this:" Griffin begins, as he clears his throat.

'Out in the far land, they who are sinners, control the land. They end life, after life, after life, only to build a quaint castle... A particular one by the name of 'Hotel Everly'.

There, they the pirates, they are the one legged, eye patched, hooked handed gang with skulls imprinted on all. Rumors say their underwear has the identical print. It is most believable.

Their plan? They will hijack the castle first. The opposing side will be tormented to tears, till the very owners will have to capitulate their sacred land, their precious castle, and gift it all to them, the pirates. After doing so, Capitan Bones, the leader of them all, will go to the undergrounds, and retrieve what he claims is his. His treasure.

All will go according to plan.

"Ahoy! Stop this madness!" Captain Bones yells, scratching his coarse beard as he orders his crew to speed up the ship, the *Foul Liberty*, his ship.

Through his different colored eyes, he can spot the land. His rival's land.

In a matter of time they manage to reach the land, lurching off their beloved ship, and making their way into the castle. Once inside, Captain Bones' plan is already ruined. Or as he would say: "My plan! It is derelict!"

The rivals had been expecting them. The rivals were not only prepared to the bone, but, they were anxiously ready to fight, to begin combat.

Face to face with them no-gooders, they don't stand a chance! Is what Captain Bones presumed. In doing so, he insolently takes out his extensive sword.

"Pirateers, it is time to take back what is ours! Charge!" he commands.

Swords pierce through the air. Clink! Clank! Again, and again, the rivals stop their swords. Eventually, the pirates manage to penetrate through the opposition's soft skin. Blood pouring out, rushing, gushing, cascading. Punches stab through the air. Kicks and spins. Yells and moans.

"Argh!"

Others are launched against walls, crushed as they collapse, blanked out. Clenching onto another's collar punch after punch. Kicks and kicks. Vases and decorations subside, slicing into flesh. Grunts and grinding of teeth. Different blood splatters onto clothes, it's nasty smell invading the air. Charging and stomping over bodies, into the swarm of more and more fighters. A second round approaches Captain Bones and his crew but he's not worried. Again they slice their way to treasure.

"Blimey! We did it." he cheers, chuckling. He and his crew don't waste any time; they charge into the underground frontier of the castle. Captain Bones' treasure awaits.

There it is! He has spotted it. His precious chest! A silver-framed, blue coated, wooden chest, with a lock the size of his heart. He impatiently grabs his key from his locket, which he keeps around his broad neck. He opens the chest, with anticipation. Nonetheless, he is greeted by skeletons, spider webs, and the lively scent of nothingness. Wildly, he thrusts all of the skeletons to the side, as they clatter against one another. Nothing!

"Arghh!" he propels his boot against the hard wall. "How can this be?"

"These aren't tales, these are true," I hear Scarlet announce.

"Huh? I hadn't finished reading," Griffin pouts.

"I've been to the 'underground frontier', it's the basement of the 'castle', of the hotel," she explains, in her soft, ever-so piping voice.

"What were you doing there?" Griffin asks her.

"Let me finish…there are endless amounts of skeletons, and…" Sarah begins explaining.

"What were you doing there?" Renata requests.

"I saw a chest," Scarlet continues, ignoring Renata.

"What were you doing there?" Samuel yells, I assume he is thinking the same theory as I am. "Thinking of hiding Allen's body in there?"

"I - What?" They are still coming at her, attacking her, like sharks surging the bait. Regardless, I'm not so certain that Samuel has thought this all through. The perplexity inside of me swirls like flames as I sway my body closer to the door to place my eye to the peephole. I crave to observe it all.

"You heard me, did you not? Let me repeat it. You…" Samuel hollers as he irascibly jolts up from his armchair.

"Oh, please! It wasn't me, I didn't kill him, Samuel," Scarlet responds, she is so done with all the accusations. "Get that inside your little head."

"Okay, okay. But you can't ignore the fact that every single clue points to you," Samuel shouts.

"Like?" Scarlet smirks.

"Bandana," Samuel begins.

"The fake 'he loved you, you didn't love him,'" Griffin points out.

"Your room is room twenty-three," Samuel says.

"Um... your point?" Scarlet queries, as she keeps a steady gaze upon Samuel's face. Her face painted red in disgust.

"Am I the only one who thought of this?" Samuel asks, as he looks at the rest of them around the room. At last he moves his gaze upon Renata. He looks at Renata, she looks down at her feet. It's like dominoes. She knows. She knows but she says nothing, nothing whatsoever.

"What does the room number have to do with anything?" Pierre now asks, his back is towards me, he is extremely tense.

"Well, my smart Pierre..." Samuel jokes, as his eyes squint in anger. "Room twenty-three is right on top of room thirteen, which means they share the emergency outside exit, the one by the window."

"So?" Scarlet shouts, interrupting him, it is evident that Scarlet knew about this.

"Let me finish! What is this hypocrisy?" Samuel roars, as he digs his nails into his palm. The rest of them get a sharp, electric shock at the raising of his voices.

"Excuse me?" Scarlet now stands as she approaches Samuel and tries to punch him. He dodges the punch. Pierre grabs Scarlet by the waist and pulls her down, forcing her to sit, as she tries again and again to get up.

"Hear me out," Samuel says, in a slow whisper. "You killed Allen, which we already established. You ran up to your room, to make others think that you were simply in your room and instead you wanted to grab his dead body and bring him to the basement, where nobody would find him."

"No!" she pleads, as she tries to slap Pierre's arm away. "No!"

"Except, as you were about to do that, you heard Griffin in the shower and decided to leave Allen, to frame Griffin. And you stayed with Pierre, so that it seemed as if you were out with him and away from the crime scene," Samuel explains, as he tries to keep his

voice steady.

Woah! Not even, I, a wise old man - or so I wish to be - hadn't thought of that. Samuel is by all means the most intelligent of the bunch. They have all turned their heads to face Scarlet, her cheeks steaming, her skin boiling with rage.

"No, no that's not true," her voice is shaky.

"Yes, yes it is." Samuel continues saying.

"Please, no you're scaring me," she cries.

"Me? I'm scaring you?" Samuel roars with laughter. "You're hilarious, Scarlet," he scoffs.

After another good ten minutes of bickering and rebukes, I hear their footsteps approach the door. I quickly hide away behind a door as they exit the library. I watch as they leave, and as they do I decide to head back to the cabin for some much needed rest.

Just as I pass by the room, I hear Griffin and Samuel still in the room. What are they still doing in the room? I decide to stay. To listen. I want to know what they say. I need to know.

"Sam?" Griffin whispers.

"Yeah?" he answers.

"Please tell me what happened that night," Griffin pleads.

"Okay, I will. It's not as if you're blackmailing me or anything," Samuel snarls.

"Just begin," Griffin instructs.

"I had just won the championship of water polo, around early September. Allen and I went out to celebrate, to a bar near his house. On the way he kept congratulating me, he insisted we celebrate. I was happy. So was he. He was happy when I was happy.

Weeks after, I had won the trophy for most improved, in my musical group. Still Allen congratulated me. We celebrated. We were happy.

Months passed and all was well, until one night when my roommate, William Gold, you've met him before, showed me the college's daily newspaper. I had submitted a poem that I wrote to a competition. Again, Allen was there for me. Supportive and all.

But all in all, he wasn't supportive. He was, but I felt pity telling him my achievements.

I felt uncomfortable, telling my dreams, my achievements to a small-minded person."

"Are you saying -" Griffin interrupts him. Samuel, doesn't complain but, continues explaining, in his story-telling tone: high-pitched, in a victim sort of way.

"It was days after the competition had terminated that I found out that he'd been chosen too, for the competition at the literary fair. He'd given up his spot for me," Samuel stops, he recollects his breath, and leans forward.

"How did you know? That he gave up his spot for you, I mean?" Griffin asks him.

"I heard him talking to Ms. Anderson, after class. Once he exited the class, I started asking him why he would do that - because everyone has a small part of selflessness, and that's normal. So I was bewildered when I heard Allen had given up his spot in the competition for me, without anything in return.

Allen simply argued that he wouldn't even get acknowledged by anyone, if he were to win. Plus, he wasn't proud of his work. He wanted me to grow into a love for literature.

I don't even like writing! I wrote the poem in five minutes, on the way to class.

Nonetheless, I had left it at that.

Again, weeks passed, he and I went out to dinner and we meet this elderly man, with an incredibly circular face, by the name of Johnson."

"Are you serious! *The* Johnson?" Griffin exclaims.

"Yeah... I didn't know he was the judge of the fair. Allen, to my right, was going insane..." Samuel explained.

"No kidding."

"We chatted some, and Allen ended up telling him about the two spots, and how I 'took' the only available slot. Johnson asks Allen if he could read his poem out of curiosity, in exhilaration, Allen agrees eagerly, as he pops it up on his phone.

After he's finished reading…"

"What?" Griffin requests.

"The judge was in tears," Samuel finally says.

"Johnson? The Johnson, was in tears?"

"Yeah."

"He's a professional…" Griffin trails off. "What was the poem about?"

"About me," Samuel explains.

"You?"

"Yes. I read Allen's poem after the judge had done so." Samuel explains. "It was about how - how unsupportive Allen felt he was, but he still tried. Because he wanted me to succeed, rather than himself. Because, he felt himself always as a minor character, he's always had a minor role, in MY shadows. He expressed how it was easier to show empathy and celebration for me, rather than go through the process of endeavor and failure himself. 'Lack of confidence, rejection, failure. Me.' is how it ends."

"Oh," Griffin gasps, as he places his hand over his mouth. I observe through the crack of the half-closed door. "He's always been self-conscious. About his emotional status, as well as his physical appearance, you know? Such a shame."

Samuel nods, in confession.

"Johnson just comments 'I hope your friend knows what an extraordinary friend he has', and walks away," Samuel continues.

"Well, does he? Do you?" Griffin asks him.

"No! No, Griffin, I don't," Samuel cries. "I was angry, bro! I wanted to know what he thought sometimes. I don't want to be told crap. I wish he had told me how he felt, I wished I could've made his life a little better. I want him to succeed but, he told me what was the point of succeeding, if nobody cared. If nobody knew. I was furious. I am furious. Because… because he died, without us making amends."

As the last sentence tumbles off his tongue, Samuel tries to rush out of the room, as Griffin's big bicep stops him.

"I'm sorry," Griffin sighs, apologetically.

"He said a couple of words, that…"

"That what?" Griffin questions.

"That kind of shot me to the heart. He said, that he was happy when I was. Sad, when I was sad. He respected me when I felt at my lowest. Celebrated when I was feeling on top of the roof. Only because…only because he could never, would never, experience that variety of emotions. But he told me that I was miserable. That it turned me into a selfish, self-centered person. That I had some nerve to judge him. To demonstrate to him, his flaws," Samuel carries on. "Griffin, that's how I am. I can't be fake. I can't hold a mask over my face. That's why only a couple of people enjoy being with me. And I'm okay with that, I am. But, not from Allen, not from him. He was what brought a smile to my face, almost every day. Every single day. And now, not only his judgement, but also himself - he's gone."

"I'm sorry." Is all Griffin can say.

"A couple weeks back, he had just started opening up to me. All his goals, his midnight hobbies. He liked to draw, he liked to write. Yes, there was still that part of me that was mad, annoyed even, at him. But for that couple of hours, I'd put it aside, for a while. He was surprised, when he found out I had no idea he liked to draw, or write, or snowboard.

'You know I'm not good with words, not out loud at least. I thought you'd known me long enough to know that by now' he had told me. Yes, I was blind. But he was mute."

"I'm…"

"It was too much, Griffin. Too much." his voice is shaky now, like a palm tree in a demolishing hurricane. "All the pity, the guilt. It was overbearing. It was unhealthy."

"Sam, did you…?" Griffin speaks tentatively.

"Did I what?" Samuel asks.

"Did you kill him?" Griffin continues, whispering almost as if the words are prohibited.

"Of course not," Samuel hollers. He inhales deeply and walks towards the door. "Are you happy? Now that you know? Or am I now a possible threat, a killer?"

The night crawled its way towards the hotel, as the moon's light peaks through the trees. I chuckle as I imagine the moon and the trees playing hide-and-seek.

The evening had passed as fast as it came and the atmosphere during dinner wasn't the best. Renata, stated she didn't want to stay in the room with Scarlet, complaining that she is a potential murderer. Scarlet wants to drink and forget. Samuel wants to call the cops. Pierre suggests he calls his older sister over to the hotel, to help them solve all this chaos. Griffin sits in his usual spot, calm and collected, as always.

They tease him, that he was at the scene of the crime and that he can't have the liberty card.

But in the end, they are all weary of this. All of this. They bicker and tease and argue, because they want to figure out this puzzle and stop all the stress. They want to build a dam with all the rocks which keep collapsing on top of them, in generous, bountiful amounts.

At the end of dinner, another wave crashes over them:

"I'd like to say something," Griffin announces, he stutters once all eyes turn to him.

Nobody responds, and he takes it as a sign to continue.

"I'd like to get to the bottom of this. We can't go home, so why not make use of the time? I want to know what happened to my best friend. And I need everyone to pitch in, because I want to figure this out. And if nobody is willing to confess, then I'll just figure it out myself." The rest of them observe him in an aloof manner.

"First, I'm going to start with…" he looks around the room, he and Scarlet make the first eye contact. "Scarlet."

Again, nobody says anything.

"You, have Allen's bandana," he begins coolly. "You faked Allen's love for you."

"I approve," Samuel finally joins in when it suits him.

"After considering everything, it is quite obvious you faked it," Samuel speaks in a professional manner, teasing Griffin in a way. "So why'd you do it?"

Scarlet doesn't say anything. Instead she closes her eyes in desperation, and shakes her head.

"We're waiting," Samuel teases, as waits for Scarlet to come up with her answer.

"No," Pierre speaks up, as he takes a sip of his water. "No."

"No, what?"

"No," Pierre repeats. "Scarlet didn't lie about anything."

"How do you know?" Samuel responds, defensively.

"Because," Pierre begins saying, as he takes a short breath.

"Are you seriously going to defend her again, Pierre? This is insane," Renata gasps.

"Come on! Own up to the facts sitting right under your nose," Samuel adds. "She made up the love story, she said she stole the bandana for remembrance, when it was actually what she used to hold the knife that killed Allen, so that no fingerprints would show. She was even thinking of hiding poor Allen in the basement - the guy you knew since preschool. Preschool, Pierre! She wanted to hide him in the basement, to let him rot there."

"If you let one more word exit your mouth I swear I'll…" Scarlet stands.

"You'll what? Kill me too?" Samuel smirks, his arms crossed across his mustard yellow sweater. He's so convinced it's her. Maybe too convinced.

"Okay, stop. Stop." Pier shouts. "Allen loved Scarlet, to such an extent that it was scary. He was obsessed with her. And I know this, *Samuel*, because I was there to experience it with Scarlet, long before Allen died." Pierre explains, as tears flow into his eyes, like wine into a glass.

It was as if Samuel had gotten a blow to the face, but I was wrong. His whole mindset quickly shifted.

"Oh. Oh, I'm sorry Scarlet. Your boyfriend here is the one who killed Allen." Samuel shouts.

"Samuel, maybe we should…" Renata begins saying as she looks at Pierre's sorrowful eyes.

"I can't deal with you anymore Samuel. I can't." Pierre sobs, his tears blurring his vision as he stomps out of the room. "If only you'd experience what Scarlet had to go through." Seconds later, Scarlet does the same, like a duckling following it's mother.

Even I felt this to be too much.

The day felt long and tiring, so I decided to go immediately to bed in the hope that I would avoid thinking. Because, once I start thinking, it seems practically impossible to stop.

It's around 3 am, when I hear a voice calling out.

Griffin! Griffin! Griffin! Three times, it calls in a strong prominent voice. As I try to get up, in my sleep-like state, is when it hits me. Like jumping dozens of meters into water. This has happened before… some dozen nights before. Can it possibly be that Griffin is communicating with someone from outside the hotel? I once again light my candle and hold it to my bedroom window. Nothing is outside, only the night and its creatures: crickets, wasps, birds, and owls. The stars in the sky, and the fireflies play games in the grass.

Nevertheless, I am awoken again. By my nightmares. I go downstairs into the kitchen for a glass of milk and as I do so, I hear Pierre and Scarlet by the front entrance doors.

"Please don't go, please," Pierre is warning her.

"Come with me." Scarlet proposes, she's got a flimsy bag over her right shoulder and her hair loose over the other.

"No. You know I can't." Pierre responds, sternly.

"Then I guess this is goodbye, Pierre," Scarlet sighs.

"No! I will tell the others."

"So? I will be gone by then," Scarlet shrugs.

"But, you've got nowhere to go, S. There's trees and trees for ages. You could die out there."

She sighs in response.

"It's better than staying in here," she gestures to the hotel.

"Just come back, S. There's no point in leaving. I promise, we'll leave soon, together," Pierre pleads, his eyes wide.

She finally gives in, so I approach them.

"What's going on?"

"Oh, nothing," they smile in sync as they make their way past me and up the stairs.

Chapter seven

It's so pleasant to wake up with the sun. The golden rays blanket the clouds and meadows with bright, intriguing colors. It feels so confident. So motivating. So bold. Golden.

As I approach the kitchen to prepare breakfast for my guests, I stop as I look once again at *her* chair.

She coos, and opens her tooth-less mouth. It turns into a sort of crooked smile and it makes my day.

I'm in the best mood I could ever ask for: the hotel has reopened after years and years of closure and I have my daughter right by me. Myla looks at me with her pure, dark ocean eyes. It was only months ago that Thalia had a round belly.

I hear the kitchen door swing open, as Ophelia strolls into the room.

"There's my most lovely grandma!" I announce, with an ear to ear grin.

"I'm your only grandma," she smirks as she picks up Myla from where she had been seated.

"Yes well," I falter, as she kisses me on the cheek.

"I'm here for Myla, you get back to work," she declares as she indicates the food roasting in the oven. She begins to saunter out, with Myla in her strong arms.

"Hey, Ophelia?" I call out, as she looks back at me.

"Yes?" she responds, turning her neck, in an elegant motion.

"I know you've told me a lot of times. But Myla hasn't heard the story," I hinted. She already knows what I am referring to.

"Larry, not right now," she sighs.

"I have a right to hear it again, don't I?" I plead, playing the innocent card.

"Of course you do, darling, but you have work to do. The dining room is packed with people," she explains but she lets go of the door and comes back inside the kitchen.

"Please?" I beg.

"Okay, if you insist," she sighs, sitting down on Myla's chair. While Myla closes her eyes, snug in her lap. She knows well by now, I'm too stubborn to fight with. "Well, I found you in the forest, alone. Wrapped in a rag. Can I tell you- Myla... the quick story?" she inquires.

"Well, okay," I give in. While both Ophelia and I know that it is me who wants to hear my story over and over again. Even though I have memorized it by now, and written it in eight different diaries, I still feel this satisfaction in hearing it every time.

"You cried alone, in the forest, in the deadly forest. Wolves were surrounding you when I heard your shrieking cry. The shrieking cry.

"I luckily got there in time, and saved you. Once I bathed you and fed you, I realized you weren't a newborn. You were about two or three years old. I was already thirty at the time, so I thought it would be difficult to raise you. However, you got on my good side, so, I decided to teach you all I know, and..." she starts saying.

"Ophelia?" I request.

"Now that I think about it, I don't know why I made you call me grandma... At first I felt guilty to try and replace your birth mother, but she's the one who left you in the woods to die in the first place" *she continues saying, her eyes closed, as though she were thinking right back to that exact moment.*

"Thank you again, Ophelia, for saving me. For everything," I thank her. "And thanks for letting me hear the story, again."

"You don't have to thank me every time I tell you the story," she jokes, her eyes now half-opened.

"Ophelia?" I request for the second time.

"Yes?" she responds, as she rocks Myla soothingly in her arms.

"Did he ever see me? Have I ever met him?" I question.

"No," she spits out, in an instant.

"Oh, so, when you started training me to work at the hotel, he was never... " she cuts me off.

"No he... Arthur died one month before I found you, when we were ambushed," she explains. "When the hotel was invaded."

Hold up - Arthur? My grandma's ex-lover is Arthur? The diary is Arthur's. But Arthur is alive isn't he? He wrote in the diary that he managed to survive. My mind thirsts to know more.

I place my hand in my back pocket, and hear my wallet clatter against my Swiss pocket knife. Where are my keys? Then I remember I don't even have a car anymore. Poor Jesse.

"Larry? Where are you going?" Renata asks me as she sees me sprinting out of the kitchen and exiting out of the dining room doors.

"Nowhere," I sigh, recalling I lost my Jesse.

"I've been meaning to ask you if Pierre's sister can come here for a few days?" she wonders.

"I- I don't think extra guests would be a good idea…"

"Only for a day or two," she pleads.

"I don't know," I say, recalling what they had said the previous day: Pierre's sister is a detective. If the story gets out, it will be terrible for the hotel's reputation.

"Oh please! She's driving all the way here for just two days." she pouts, as she extends her lower lip.

"Why would she come here?" I stupidly ask. I want to know if she has the courage to lie to me. To my face.

"Um, she wants to visit Pierre." Liar.

"Wait, she's driving here?" I ask, remembering she said something about driving. Driving equals car. Maybe my thirst will be quenched.

"Yes. It's insane. She's driving all alone in a tiny car for hours and hours. Just to come here." she explains.

"I guess she really misses Pierre, huh?" I say, with narrow eyes.

"Yea…" Lie to me a third time, Renata, and I will make hell rise on earth.

"Okay, I suppose she can come," I respond, with a clipped voice.

"Thank you! Thank you!" she cheers, as I look into her obsidian eyes, and drift away. A half grin painted on my face.

"Breakfast is served," I announce as I give them each pancakes, showered in syrup, or drizzled in powdered sugar.

"Great, thanks!" they exclaim. I then do, as I have done previously, for every single meal: I 'walk off'. Except they don't know I'm hidden under the dining room stage, where the musicians used to play. Here I can hear all. Here I can see all.

"Pierre, when is your sister coming?" Scarlet asks him.

"In five days' time, I believe," he responds. While he takes a sip of his tea, soaked in sugar. So sweet. For his bitter heart.

"Okay, what do we do till then?" Renata questions.

"Till then… nothing. We will wait for her," he says.

"What other evidence do we have?" Griffin questions, as more of an ice breaker rather than out of curiosity. They all look at him, had he already forgotten what happened last time?

"I'm so curious as to why you are all so calm. There is a killer amongst us." Samuel exclaims. "How are you guys so calm?"

"I have to agree with Samuel," Renata agrees.

"Because I'm not seated next to the killer," Scarlet responds coolly, deadly staring at Samuel who is seated diagonally from her.

"May I make a suggestion?" Pierre cuts in, pointing his finger in the air. "I did some analyzing last night, after dinner and…"

"Yes?" Renata responds as the rest of them stare at him.

"Has it ever occurred to any of you that… Allen was killed?"

"Yes," Samuel smirks, chuckling. What a clown.

"Let him finish." Renata exclaims.

"That Allen killed himself?" Pier announces. His eyes rest in his hands.

The words struggle in suspension through the air.

"I-no," they respond, in a chorus.

"He would never," Griffin practically whispers. I find it so hard to understand what's happening when Griffin speaks, he's a quiet, sly fox.

"But did you really know him all that well?" Pier asks.

"Yes!" Griffin exclaims.

"I would've never thought that one of us is a killer, but again, here we are," Samuel responds.

"That…" Renata begins to say, but stops herself.

"But if he killed himself, that doesn't make him a killer," Scarlet argues. "If he decided to end his life, why should he be called a killer?"

"Because if he did, which I'm not certain of…" Samuel responds, glaring directly at Scarlet. "He's extremely selfish."

"How dare you say that," Scarlet shouts. "If he was suffering and-"

"Stop acting so sensitive!" Samuel argues.

"Samuel calm down," Pierre tells him. "Please."

"No, I can't calm down. Don't tell me what to do," he shouts, as he makes his glass fall to the floor. It shatters to pieces, as the juice sprints into the carpet floor, staining it.

"Why was it selfish?" Renata questions, potentially interested in Samuel's point of view.

"It was selfish. It was selfish, because instead of ending his pain, he passed it to others!" Samuel shouts, as I take a look at his eyes. They slowly start to become more bloodshot than they already were, first from the lack of sleep, the stress, the confusion. Now, it's because he is about to cry. As my prediction is confirmed, his lips tremble a bit and he inhales a short breath. And he lets it all out. Tears flowing down his cheeks like rivers rushing down mountains. His hands grasping his hair, he screams uncontrollably.

This conversation was kept on hold till they got back to their rooms, one or two hours later. I sprinted home, to continue listening through my headphones. I'm extremely surprised they haven't found the bug yet. These high-tech things, it's crazy how they work! If only this extreme technology existed when I was a kid...

"If we wish to continue having this conversation, we have to all stay calm," Griffin says, the rest of them agree.

"Can it really be that he killed himself?" Scarlet wonders.

"Yes, yes it can," Renata responds, with sorrow.

"Where was the stab mark?" Samuel asks. He's onto something.

"Under his ribcage," Griffin responds.

"To the right?" Samuel questions, although it sounded more like a comment.

"Yes," Griffin approves.

"Okay so he didn't kill himself," Samuel concluded. His voice is now clearer, he seems relieved.

"How do you know?" Pierre cuts in.

"Everyone pick up a pencil," he instructs them. I hear clattering through my headphones. "Just as I thought."

"What do you mean?" Griffin asks.

"You all picked up the pencil with your right hand. Allen was left handed," Samuel explains.

"Exactly. To end his life, he had to stab on the right side, since he was a lefty," Pierre argued. He sounds so confident, as if he has outsmarted Samuel.

"You see, that's what the real killer wants you to think," Samuel explains, as I smirk, imagining Pierre's deluded face. "To get out of it easily, he made it seem as if Allen killed himself, so the killer stabbed on the right side. That's also why the cut wasn't the deepest."

"What do you mean?" Pierre asks.

"Must I really explain everything? Even the most obvious?" Samuel sighs deeply. "Since one of us killed Allen with their left hand, which is our weak hand, the killer didn't have that much strength. However, that weak stab was enough to kill our poor friend."

"-And on the other hand, Allen would have been stronger, so if he had killed himself, the cut would have been deeper," Renata thinks out loud.

"Or," Samuel continues. "The cut was shallow, to try and prove that Allen did it to himself. That Allen didn't have enough power. But you see, I could see right through that scheme. Quite frankly, it's basic."

"So the question remains, who killed Allen?" Scarlet concludes, as she can't help but stare at Samuel. Guilty of murder, in her opinion.

"The sinner sure was good at hiding their tracks," Pierre sighs.

I decide to take some time to think.

But I don't want to stay alone with my thoughts. I go to my bedroom to search for Arthur's diary. I must talk to him, I need to talk to Arthur, if he's still alive that is... If Ophelia found me when she was thirty, and I was around three years old... That means, hypothetically thinking, that he is now around one hundred years old. Hopefully he hasn't passed away, like Ophelia did. There's a slither of hope, and it's enough to persuade my mind...until my mind sinks deep into my memories once again.

The worst day of my life. June 30th. Time 1:22 am.

Months ago, a disease approached the world. The Foul Giddie. It generates abnormal heat across the body. If cooled too much, the body would shut down, till one turns to a frozen, soul-less statue. On the other hand, if the body is not cooled enough, the body will overheat to such an extent that the heat can pass to others, infecting others with the disease. This is of course, in the worst cases.

Mild cases include, simple fevers, sniffles, or headaches. Unfortunately, neither Ophelia nor Thalia had mild cases, they had severe cases of the Foul Giddie. Myla, who is at the age of eleven, was extremely frightened for the well-being of the family.

Ophelia comes home one night, from a nearby hospital, in which she helps out five days a week, and comes home for the weekends. She absolutely loves helping others, no matter the risk. She comes home that night, the eternal sky behind her. That promising sky, luminous sky, sparkled with opals and wonders beyond the human mind, blanketed with a velvet darkness, which strangely felt so immensely safe.

We have dinner together, and afterwards Ophelia insists she tells us a story. The table is cleared, and all that is left are coffee mugs, which sit, with gracious steam.

Ophelia is about mid-story as she takes a sip of her coffee.

"How long did you boil the water for, Larry?" she asks me. "It's burning."

"Same as always," I respond, sipping the coffee, as I catch one of the marshmallows flowing into my mouth.

"What's wrong with your coffee?" Thalia asks her.

"Nothing dear, it's just extremely hot," she explains. "I'll just wait for it to cool down some more." Just as she finishes her sentence, Myla takes a sip of Ophelia's coffee.

"Myla! How many times have I told you to not drink coffee? Especially your grandma's," Thalia scolds her.

"Oh, my! Don't worry about these silly things," Ophelia smiles.

"But ma, the coffee is practically cold!" Myla states.

"Pass it here let me have a taste," I say, as I take a sip of the coffee, all their eyes on me. "She's right." I approve, as a frigid bitter taste runs down my throat.

Thalia knows exactly what to do, for she was a nurse in her previous times. She places her lips to Ophelia's forehead.

"She's burning!" She announces. "Bring her to her bed, Myla!"

As soon Myla does as she is told, I look at Thalia's face. Her poker face.

"What is it?" I ask her, as I see her gathering a few things.

"Eh-" she begins saying, while grabbing a towel. I try to read her face, which does not reveal any expression, and indication as to what she might be thinking.

"Thalia! What is it?" I exclaim, as she keeps grabbing more and more items.

"Keep your voice down, Larry. She's got the Foul Giddie," she responds, solemnly. She looks at me, and she stops picking out items for a split second. "Don't worry, Larry. I will cure her. I promise."

"What do you need?" I inquire, as my mind starts to present itself of all the worst case scenarios. "Should we take her to the hospital?"

"No! The hospital is a place where infected people are all dumped at. You can't be serious?" Thalia snaps, as items practically cascade down her arms. Like a dam, being overfilled with water.

"Oh, okay," I respond. "Sorry."

"Bring me ice, a wet rag, and water," she implores.

"Will you cool her?" I question.

"Yes, I presume so," Thalia tells me, as she heads over to where Ophelia is at.

Once I gather a bucket of ice, a wet rag, and a jug of water, I bring the items to the bedroom where she lies. I see Thalia at her side, while Myla on the other.

"Here," I announce, while placing them by Thalia's side.

"I will not cool her," she informs me, just as I finish placing down the heavy bucket of ice.

"Why not?!" I exclaim. I must confess, I'm quite concerned.

"Because, although I haven't been trained or taught precisely for this particular moment. After having observed her, and her physical state, I find that there is a more likely chance that she will," she pauses. "pass away, if we cool her."

"But..." I argue.

"Larry, listen to her!" Ophelia groans.

"Okay, okay," I give in.

"We can only hope for the best: that she won't overheat," Thalia says, more to herself. She inhales slowly and exhales even slower.

After extended hours of anticipation Thalia speaks:

"You and Myla wait outside, and don't come back inside, unless I tell you to do so," Thalia tells us.

"But why?" Myla argues, as she holds onto Thalia's forearm.

"Come on Myla!" I shout, as I try to pull her free.

"It's because since her temperature is rising constantly, she is at the point where she can pass the disease to us," Thalia explains to Myla, in a false comforting smile.

"But how will you protect yourself ma?" Myla asks her.

"I'm strong, honey. Now go with your father," Thalia responds as Myla finally decides to let go of Thalia's arm. Thalia looks at me and grins. She nods her head, indicating that I must leave now.

It's around 1:22 am, when Myla finally falls asleep. I decide to go check on Thalia, for she may need my help caring for Ophelia.

"Thalia I'm coming in," I announce, as I don't wait for a response.

What I find behind that door, it's indescribable. It's like my whole entire being comes subsiding on top of me, compressing me to the floor. Bulldozing me against the wall of nothing, full force, no heads up. Disintegrates me. Demolishes my soul, whole.

Thalia is now on the floor, covered in ice. Damp rags on her face. Water dashing through her hair. Her face is completely pale. Her eyebrows are full of petite icicles. Her lips dry.

Then I look at Ophelia. On the bed, her face filled with tiny, sweat drops. The top of her hair, wet. Her clothes, all drenched. Her bedsheets, humid. The thermometer under her arm runs red throughout the tube.

Both gone. Both...

"No, no, no," I put my head on Thalia's beat-less chest.

"No! Please, no!" I wail. I throw the chair at the wall and it falls. To pieces. Bursting. I thrust all the vases, all the picture frames off the dresser. They collapse. Glass shattering. Everywhere. "God please!"

I grab a rag from the floor and pull it, as hard as I can. It tears in two, as one of the pieces falls onto the candle. The rag starts to be dominated by ferocious flames. My eyes burn with pain.

"Dad!"

"Dad!" I hear the door open. Myla is awake. I turn to look at her. She's petrified. Completely petrified.

Sweat trickles down my temple, as tears crack down my face, my arms shake, uncontrollably, as my feet give in and I collapse to the ground. I black out.

It was evident what had happened. Thalia had been infected by the disease, as Ophelia overheated. In order to try and save herself, Thalia quickly laid on the floor, by trying to cool herself down, in all ways possible. But in the end, both methods ended in the deaths of two of my favorite people in the world. At least I still have Myla.

Two weeks later she ran away.

I felt trapped in this massive spider web, constructed of all my emotions. Cemented by all my memories, the events which manufactured my life, my actions, my choices.

For years I had completely shut down. I was scared to look at myself in the mirror, because I couldn't bear the feeling of not knowing the man one the other side of the mirror. Maybe I still am, maybe I still am filled with horrors. Because the guilt that overtakes my nerves each time I look at myself is too much. Too much for my mind to control. To manipulate, to regulate even. The what ifs that race their way across my head, like rolling rocks, down a mountain. A steep mountain.

What if I had checked on Thalia earlier? Would I
have saved a life? What if I protested and stayed
with Thalia all night? Would I have prevented it all?
Or would I have died myself? Would that have been
better?

<u>Chapter eight</u>

It's around mid-morning when I hear the group squabble once more, in the dining room.

"My my, quite the manipulator we got here, eh?" Scarlet says in a sing-song voice.

"I'm telling you, I don't know why he had my father's knife!" Samuel exclaims, as I hear his fists catapult onto the table.

"Well, guess what?" Scarlet slowly responds, with a pause. "I don't believe you."

"What's going on?" I decide to approach the situation, this time. "Oh my days!"

The knife is placed in the center of the table. I'd never seen it before, but the blood stain on the tip indicates all. The pommel, is a triangular shape, in a melanite hue. Leather seems to be the material. The smooth leather which makes up the bottom of the knife, has a capital 'J' embossed into it with eye-catching rubies. The blade, immensely sharp and long. A particular design flows on the side of the blade, until the dried blood devours it.

"Why do you kids carry that knife?" I ask, taken-aback.

"It's Samuel's," Scarlet accuses, eyeing Samuel, as he quickly grabs the knife and hides it from my view.

"Well, Samuel, why do you have that knife?" I request, in a concerning tone. I'm ready to shake things up. Get some chaos rippling.

"It's not my knife!" Samuel exclaims. I look at him from the corner of my eye, just enough for him to feel my gaze upon him. Like a lighthouse, in a drowner's inaudible call.

"It has a 'J' on it, though," I recall, as I can sense Scarlet's smile approaching her voice. She sure loves when people are on her side.

"You see Samuel? Anyone could tell it is yours," She smirks, as she rolls her bossy eyes. Her heart is practically beating out of her chest, her keenness to be right, is violently ear-piercing.

"Samuel, bro-" Griffin starts to give in.

"It's not my knife. It's my- it's my, my pa's," he shouts.

"Then why do you have it?" I inquire, in a scolding voice.

"Because," he pauses, while he looks around at the rest of them. "I don't know, alright?"

"Did your dad make that?" Pierre asks, joining the conversation. I wonder why Renata is so quiet. She's more of a listener, I suppose.

"Yes, he blade smiths, and crafts the pommel of daggers, knives…" he explains. "He owns a little shop, in town, back home."

"Yes?" I question, in doubt.

"I'm not sure about it either, Larry," Scarlet adds, she shrugs her shoulders.

"Why have you never told us this?" Griffin asks.

"Yes, exactly. It makes it much less believable," Renata finally subsides. Just when I was beginning to think that there are some sort of 'alliances' going on. I guess not.

"The fact that Allen killed himself with this knife, means a lot," Pierre begins saying, in a slow voice.

Like a predator waiting to pounce on his prey.
"Don't you think?"

"Yes, but-" Samuel stutters.

"Couldn't it be that *you* stole this knife from your dad's, to you know?" Pierre hypothesizes. Or is it a conclusion?

"No!" Samuel shouts.

"Afterwards you tried, in multiple failing ways to frame my girlfriend?" Pierre continues.

"I didn't frame anybody," Samuel exclaims. I can feel the walls closing in on him.

"So that's what you're telling yourself now?" Pierre requests.

"Stop!" Samuel shouts as he stands, and runs off.

"You sure don't like it when the tables are turned, do you?" Pierre screams, while Samuel runs out the door.

Then they all look at me. It hits them like a shot to the head: they have openly revealed to me information about Allen's death.

"It's about a videogame," Renata explains, in urgency.

"Videogame?" I question.

"Yes, yes," Pierre says so quickly, I had barely time to blink.

"Yes, okay," I answer. "When is your sister coming?"

"Um," he stops in his tracks. "How did you know?"

I look at Renata and I see her worried gaze. Maybe she wasn't supposed to ask me.

"Overheard you by accident," I respond, falsely.

"She's coming today," he responds.

"Any idea how long her stay will be?" I question.

"Two or three days, I presume," he responds.

"Alright," I nod my head.

"It is okay? Is it not?" he asks. "I just thought since you overheard about it and didn't say anything…"

"Yes, of course," I respond. I add a smile, while I say, "No worries."

"Perfect," he exclaims.

"We will see you later," Renata grins, as they get up from their seats and head out of the door.

"Oh. Actually, I will be out of town for a few days, for more resources. Will you all manage, without me?" I ask, in an apologetic voice. "You're not going to be alone, there's the maids and…"

"Oh yes," I see Pierre's excitement. They can freely talk about the death of Allen with no anxiety of me overhearing… Oh, if only he knew, I'd been listening all along.

"Okay…" I respond, pretending to be disappointed in his excitement.

4:30 pm. A strawberry red car approaches the hotel entrance. One could clearly see the difference between the olden beauty of the hotel and the vivid and immense energetic air of the car. Old and new.

I see an elegant-framed girl, in high boots. Her cascading, sleek and velvety cinnamon hair, swaying side to side as she skips to where Pierre and the others greet her.

"This is Leonie," I hear Pierre introduce her to the rest of the group.

Leonie says something that I can't quite comprehend, then they all exchange hugs and kisses, until they finally head inside.

No time to lose. I race inside the hotel, and just as I had hoped… Leonie has abandoned her car keys on my registration desk. I grasp them in my hand, tightly. I hop into Leonie's car. I rapidly friction my hands together with anxiousness, as I get ready to start the engine, just as I see Leonie stroll back out. I immediately get out of the car in a haste and hide behind a nearby tree. The car keys still guilty in my innocent hands.

"Forgot my luggage," she calls out to Pierre, who waits for her by the entrance.

"Where did I leave my keys?" she asks Pierre, who responds with a shrug.

"I'll just get it later," she adds, whispering to herself and heads back inside.

Perfect. Now I'll have to wait till Leonie gets her fancy bags out of the car. If not, I'll get caught and they will realize that I have stolen the car. Well, borrowed.

I wait a couple minutes before heading back inside the hotel and placing the car keys back on the counter. My plans will have to wait.

I trudge back to my cabin. I yearn for the spring to come. The snowflakes which glide through the sky will eventually reside on the frigid floor. Spring sprouts from the iced grounds, a flower, born, right where the snowflakes had fallen. The flowers evolve, with the company of the hot summer sun, into plants, or in a matter of time, trees. Fall, the leaves cascade, creating a cushion to greet the naive, fresh, snowflakes. It's beautiful.

For now, the only movement is hail crackling on the floor. Bouncing, attacking my boots. The frigid air violently brushes my cheeks, scraping them. They turn red, gelid. My dry, flakey lips, outspread their parched, desert dryness reaches into my throat. My fingertips correspond to the piercing low temperature as does my pink nose. But it's barely a fraction of what my toes feel. It's as if a numbing cream was polished over my toes, I can barely feel them when I kick them to the tree to try and feel some sort of something. I later realized what a mindless idea that was, as I took off my socks and saw my toes swelling with pain.

9:45 pm. Leonie picks up her luggage from the car. I retrieve the keys once more, from the same place she'd left them previously, and turn the engine on. It's time for me to depart. Before I do, I grasp a map from my inner pocket and mildly memorize the general direction in which I'm headed.

The car rattles on the road. The headlights illuminate the road ahead of me. Snowy mountains on the horizon, masking the radiant, celestial sky. Brilliant sparkles dotting the night.

I drive all night long. I watch the sun rise, and the moon fall. I used to think how unfortunate it was that they never met, until I experienced an eclipse. Nonetheless, before that, I'd read stories of how the sun and the moon were two lovers, who worked every single day, to keep their children alive, to keep the world functioning, to preserve life. Yet they sacrifice their own lives. Afterwards, I had interpreted eclipses as a token of gratitude, and reward for the two lovers, for watching over us. They would have that one moment where they could be united for some time, before departing their ways once again. But I didn't worry, I'd learned that an eclipse happened every so often, and they'd meet again, in some years' time. Maybe that's just how life works. And the sun and the moon are there, to show us that we shouldn't waste our time on all the planets which we greet, or maybe, if so desired, to know that we will eventually come back to our very own sun.

My hands fidget upon the steering wheel, as I realize I'm getting close to my destination. I'm torn between my curiosities, the desire to receive all the answers to my questions and nervousness. I haven't got a clue as to what might occur, in the next minutes.

I approach an old deckhouse. The wood which constructs ninety percent of the home is damp, as well as moldy. The few crammed and prison-sized windows are dusty and gray.

I park the car in the dirt and walk down the front, wilted lawn with grass patches missing here and there.

I knock on the door. From the other side of the panel, I hear footsteps approach the entryway, in a leisurely manner.

"Who is it?" a low voice requests.

"A friend of Arthur's," I decided to say, after diverse moments of contemplating this very moment on the way here.

The door opens: a lanky, extremely well-dressed man appears on the other side of the door.

"Thank you," I say, as I look at his face: a long, protruding, exaggerated nose. Small eyes, covered by dice-shaped glasses. Pale skin, adorned with a pair of thin lips. Around his forties, I suppose?

"Who did you say you were?" he questions, his back turned to me, as he wanders further into the heart of the home.

"I need to see Arthur," I explain as I follow him, although I haven't received any sort of welcome.

"Why?" He stops and finally faces me. His thin eyebrows crossed.

"Because," I take a breather. "I'm his son."

I lie, of course. I will *never* identify as his son, a man worthy of my grandma's heart should be grateful. Beholden. And what did he, Arthur do? Hide away in this- this shack, albeit with an extremely elegant interior, but that's probably beside the point.

He looks at me intensely and raises an eyebrow, it's like he's judging me as if I'm auditioning for some sort of modeling contest. Finally, he breaks eye contact and speaks once more.

"Follow me," he instructs. Wandering down the home is like strolling inside a boat: all one material and limited furniture. Polished, light wood. A minimalistic design, in regards to the living room. A couple of seating spaces and a tiny coffee table. So simple, so refreshing. Is this what modern architecture is like? Fresh? A breath of air? Yet, I can't quite grasp the sense of home, of safety. Of me.

"Your name, sir?" I ask him, as we skip through the living room.

"It's Sir Henry, to you," he snaps.

"I admire the design," I say, as I get a mhm in return.

Thankfully, finally we reach an embellished, effortless door with a bold handle.

"Arthur?" he calls, knocking on the door, at the far end of the house.

"Yes?" I hear a raspy, hoarse voice in return: he's still alive. My ultimate reassurance.

"There's someone that has come to see you!" Henry- Sir Henry announces.

"Well, bring him in, I suppose," he groans.

As Sir Henry opens the door my eyes practically roll out of my eyelids. This room is *completely* different. One word: Chaos. I've never been a particularly messy person, but this is just beyond. On the small desk, by the barred window, mountains of newspapers, magazines, books, loose papers fill the space. On the floor, good clothes thrown to the ground like rags. A skimpy twin bed in the middle of the room, with a checkered bedspread and a sky blue pillow. On the nightstand, five or six cups that previously contained tea have been packed one on top of the other. On the wall, behind the bed, a collage of blazing colors pinches my eyes. Raggedy paintings, peculiar pictographs, and hand drawn illustrations. It's all overwhelming. Not to mention, some weird stringy things attached to the ceiling, along with a broken fan, with dust icicles falling from the blades.

"Make it quick," Henry implores, as he looks at me from head to toe, once again. He squints his eyes and scoffs as he leaves, the door slams shut.

"Hello," Arthur greets, and I practically gasp as I see him. I was so caught up in the mess which he surrounds himself with, that I practically forgot there was a person in here. A someone I need to see. I need to talk to. I came here, with endless amounts of questions, accusations and it's as if I have forgotten them all, as I look at him once more.

Half of his face is carved with scars. I always thought scars told such a powerful story, that they prettified one's exterior, but I'd never seen this; faint purple, reddish color stains painted on his crackled skin, one of his eyes shut closed. Almost as if stitched together, with glue. The other eye, the lightest of colors, a gray shade to it, bloodshot, as bright red veins grow towards the pupil. Half of his lower lip is paler than the rest, bulging on the right side. Blemishes run down his neck and bubbles invade the skin under his jaw. His beard has stopped growing while ingrown hair follicles burst on the surface. His hair sprouts only in some places, white and thin.

He's in a wheelchair and not only because of old age: one of his legs is missing.

"H-hi," I respond, as a feeling of pity approaches me, I gulp it down. Remember what he did. He left Ophelia all alone. She thought he was dead for the remainder of her life. She went to heaven, thinking she'd meet him there. She…

"Stop staring, boy!" he snaps, as I retrieve my eyes and glance at my own shoes.

"Sorry, sir," I apologize.

"Well, what do you want?" he inquires.

"I'm Larry," I explain, and stop.

"Yes…?" he responds.

"I found your diary?" I announce, regardless it sounds more like a question.

"What are you talking about?" he requests.

"Your diary!" I exclaim, as I put my hand in my coat.

"What foolishness is this?" he questions, as if I'm wasting his time.

"Here," I exclaim, as I show him the diary.

"Have you stolen this, boy?" he inquires.

"No, No!" I shout.

"Then whose it?" he roars.

"It's yours. Yours," I respond, as I practically throw the diary in his lap.

"Alright, enough of this. Henry," he calls out as he shoves the diary off his lap, like a fly on a summer day.

"No, no, no. Please! Please!" I yell, as I hear Sir Henry's footsteps approach the door.

"Listen here, boy. Don't go around to old men's homes, saying these kinds of things," Arthur declares. "Henry? Take him away."

"Stop. Please. Please!" I plead as I feel Sir Henry's hands, taking control of my arms, yanking them behind my back. "Please?"

"Let's go," Sir Henry instructs, as he starts dragging me out of the room.

"I'm here because of Ophelia," I finally say, gasping for air, as Sir Henry repeatedly tries to silence me with a rag over my mouth. "Ophelia."

"What?" Arthur inquires, his eyes filled with curiosity as well as bewilderment.

"Yes. I'm her son. Please listen to me," I announce in between gasps.

"Henry let him go," Arthur immediately orders, just as I finish my sentence.

I feel Sir Henry's grasp fly away, as my knees bend and I almost fall to the floor.

"Thank you," I say anyway.

"Sit, boy," Arthur instructs, as I pick up the diary from the floor. Then, I do as he says.

"You better not be lying, boy," he remarks.

"I'm not."

"How do you know Ophelia?" Arthur inquires, impatiently. "Tell me."

"Now, calm down, sir," I exclaim. "Seconds ago, you wanted me gone."

He stares at me with uncertainty, and then lets his gaze fall upon the window: he knows I'm right. I take this time to explain:

"Ophelia, she found me in the forest. Months before you left her, or rather, 'died'" I explain, as I wait for his approval.

"How do you know this?" He interrupts. In his defense, I'd be astonished as well, if a stranger came into my home, knowing my entire life. It's insane.

"I read your diary," I answer, pointing to the diary, now on my lap.

"How dare you. It is my privacy," he yells, as he starts to get agitated. "Talking about privacy, how did you figure out where I live?"

"Sir, please allow me to finish," I request. I try to keep a hold of my patience although it tries, brutally,

to slip away. I must retrieve it. Contain myself.
Restrict myself.

"But," he utters.

"Minutes ago, you wanted me gone," I remind him, again. He seems to understand, hopefully he gets the memo this time around.

"Your address is at the end of the diary, along with your house landline. I thought I'd rather talk to you in person, rather than through a medium." I explained.

"I read your diary… multiple scenarios and circumstances did not add up," I continue. "I would like to ask you some questions."

He doesn't answer, good for him. He's beginning to learn how this works: I talk and he answers if I want him to.

"Why did you fake your death?" I inquire.

"I never faked my death. I almost died. Thankfully, I survived." He gets defensive, as he answers.

"What did you do after you survived?" I interrogate.

"Don't you know? You read the diary," He vents.

"Yes, but I want to hear it from you," I declare. How stupid, must he think I am right now.

"I went to the hospital, to take care of the burns," he's annoyed, but, doesn't show it.

"How long did you stay at the hospital?" I ask.

"Like I wrote, in *my* diary," he grumbles once more, his eyes remain bland.

I wait for him to give me a definite answer.

"Eight weeks."

"Why that long?" I remark.

"So that the wounds could heal properly," He answers, as his eyes finally speak: You know this, though.

"Did Ophelia know you survived the fire?" I stupidly ask, of course she didn't.

"Yes," he calmly responds.

"Okay, moving on…What?" This I did not know.

"Yes," he coolly repeats.

"She knew you survived?" I ask again.

"Yes, she knew I survived," he says once again. His voice starts to break. It's a crater in the busy ground.

My head starts banging and swinging, furiously, around and around. How could this be? How could this be?

"How could this be?" I hear myself say aloud, the third time.

I wait for a response… I get none.

"How could this be?" I shout, wanting an answer.

"I sent her a letter, first thing when I got out of the hospital. Telling her I was alright. Telling her I was alive," he explains. As he takes a sip out of his recent mug.

"And? What happened next?" I inquire.

"Well," he looks at me with an if-you-let-me-finish look. But his cockiness is only a mask to hide his sadness. "She wanted nothing more to do with me."

"Well why not?" I exclaim.

"'You are the most selfish man alive. You thought that by saving me, you would help me survive, leave yourself without the misery and pain of losing someone. Good for you. You accomplished that.

Your pain ended. While I paid for it. With guilt, thinking I had survived instead of you. With fright, thinking I'd live the rest of my life without you. With pain, in my heart, thinking I had lost you, forever. And I have. Lost you forever.' Her exact words. And every time, no matter how many times I reread the letter it always said the same thing," he says, as his voice is practically a whisper.

"She was angry you didn't write to her earlier?" I conclude, as more of a comment than a question.

"Not angry, oh no. Furious," he sighs. I feel so much pity for this old man. This stranger. However, I am certain Ophelia made the right choice, to say what she had to say and I'm not being biased. Why am I trying to convince myself? Why?

"What happened once you left the hospital, sir?" I calmly question, as my mind ticks and ticks. I feel like such a child. I still don't understand an adult mind. A mature mind.

"Since I had no home, I decided to make this," he gestures his arms in the air, "my home."

Has he lived here? In this little room? All alone? Only his memories for company?

"Yes, where did you happen to meet Henry?" I politely ask.

"When I was buying some supplies in a local store. Said he needed a job, so I offered him meals and a roof over his head, once my home was completed. He ended up helping me build it, as well," Arthur responds.

"I understand," I say.

A moment of silence slurred across the room, like a vicious ghost hungry for more of life. More of what could-have been. He is silenced, voiceless, by his unfulfilled life.

"How is Ophelia?" he finally questions, as he takes a load off his chest. I've been waiting for this one…

I take a moment to respond to this.

"She's great," I lie, through a wholesome, false grin.

"Good, good," he nods in satisfaction.

Is he waiting for me to ask if he wants to see her? Or- vice-versa?

"I must be going," I announce, as his tired eyes collapse in nostalgia. I don't want to make him feel any worse.

"You wouldn't want to stay the night?" He offers.

He's so lonely. So abandoned. Tears fill my eyes, as I fake a sneeze, to wipe them free. I want to be strong, for him. For Arthur. I like this man. He would've been an amazing father. Played ball with me, teach me how to draw, we'd drink beer together…

"No, no thank you. I must get back to the hotel," I respond, as I slam the door shut on my thoughts. He raises his eyebrows in awe. Dammit! He now knows the hotel is back up and running. I feel guilty for telling him such accomplishments, when he's here, all alone, waiting to die. Hoping for a better life to come.

"Yes, alright," he finally gives in.

"Sir, why did you make the diary?" I finally ask one of the many questions which stung my brain, continuously, repeatedly, till the answer would reveal itself.

"For her. For Ophelia," he responds in melancholy.

Okay, now I need to leave this place. I can't help but be reminded of Ophelia, her loving eyes. Would she have given Arthur a second chance, if she'd seen him like this?

"Oh sir, one last question?" I say, asking whether or not this would be okay.

"What is it?" He responds, in approval.

"How old are you?" I question.

"Dear me!" He chuckles, scratching his head. "Around my nineties, I suppose."

I nod, and head out the room. Regardless, I quickly turn back around, and leave the diary on his desk.

"This is yours," I pronounce.

He smiles, in response.

<u>Chapter nine</u>

I sit in the car, as for a long drive awaits. I can't help but think of how I left Arthur's room: not once glazing back. Should I have said more? Should I have told him the truth?

No, he's in his nineties. If he knew Ophelia is dead, who knows what he could've done. Killed himself to be with her? It's better never to risk it with old folks. It's strange what some do, for love. It's mindless. The mind should be stronger than your feelings, than your heart.

I vow to come back, to visit Arthur but I'm selfish. I can't bear to talk about the dead, it rubs salt in my wounds. The same ones which have been trying to heal for ages now. I can't, I won't.

Tree after tree fly by as more and more of the road gets eaten up by the car. I can only pray that nobody has noticed that Leonie's car is gone.

10:45 am. I am back home at the hotel. I venture inside the entrance hall where Renata is seated comfortably on one of the sofas reading a substantial book.

"What is it that you are reading?" I ask her, as she quickly turns her head around to see where my voice came from. "Didn't mean to scare you."

"Not at all," she grins. She places her thumb on the page to mimic a bookmark and shows me the cover. A pitch black cover, with bright gold, cursive letters 'Odyssey' was plated in the exact middle of the rectangular cover.

"Ah, a classic!" I announce, as I recall reading it when I was just a few years younger than she.

"Yes, I've read it many times before, but it still amuses me to this day," she explains.

How wonderful.

"Larry, sir," I hear Pierre call out as he and Leonie approach me. Leonie's hair, still perfect as always, not a hair misplaced. Pierre's hair has now been extremely patted down, and thoroughly gelled.

"Hello," I greet back.

"How are you?" he questions.

"I'm doing good. You must be…" I stop myself.

"Who are you?" I lie, I must play the role correctly. They don't know what I know. They don't know I stole her car. They don't know that I know her name. They don't know that I have seen her before, a couple of times actually.

"Leonie, nice to meet you," she says, her French accent lighter than Pierre's, holding out her hand for me to shake it.

"Likewise," I shake her hand, in return. "Where is everyone else?"

"In the pool, or relaxing," Pierre responds.

"Has everything been okay since I've been gone?" I question.

"Yes, yes, of course," he responds, in a reassuring nod.

"Great!" I smile back. "I'm going to go and take a shower, will you all manage till lunchtime?"

"Yes, certainly," Leonie answers instead of Pierre. Her light, upturned eyes, identical to Pierre's. As if her eyes had been copied and pasted on Pierre's face. Her eyes seem just a tad more sensitive and soft.

"I hope you all like clam chowder," I announce, as I head out. I inhale deeply.

Being back at the cabin feels great. I feel superior knowing I managed to pull off my little scheme. My lack of sleep is starting to dominate me, crawling up my spine. I must rest.

I don't waste time putting on my night robes, I simply fall onto bed and stumble into a deep sleep.

"It's not possible. You haven't checked everywhere," I rage, as I bang my fists on the countertop, as violence climbs up my palm.

"Sir, how long ago did you say your daughter ran away?" he inquires, again and again, every time I come.

And every time I come to the local sheriff station, the memory slides back into my brain. Recalling the day she left. Remembering that monumental feeling of abandonment. One moment I had it all, a family: Ophelia, Thalia, Myla. And I lost them all. I miss them so, so insanely much. It's like someone punched me in the chest, with more force each time.

It was night, right after 8 pm. I had forgotten to make dinner, so I decided to bring ice cream to Myla's room. I mount the stairs as I hear clattering from her room.

"Myla?" I had called. "What's going on?"

She didn't have time to answer before I opened the door.

"Are you leaving?" I ask, as I stupidly stare at the bag at her feet. Whereas, my feet stay planted to the ground, as if by nails.

"Yes and you can't stop me," she announces.

"Myla, honey, can we at least talk this through?" I plead, as I touch her hand, in sympathy.

"What is there to talk about?" she requests, removing her hand, from under mine. "That you've been a terrible dad? You've forgotten I exist, as I hear you stripping paintings from walls, throwing everything around, there's broken glass everywhere. You haven't eaten one meal with me in ages. In this place, I see mom everywhere. I hear Ophelia every night, in my heart. I can't deal with this anymore, Dad, I can't."

"I'm sorry, I'll be better. I promise," I pledge.

"Sorry's not enough this time," she responds, avoiding my eyes.

"Why not?" I shout, my voice now raspy and parched.

"Because, Dad, you can't even take care of yourself. How do you expect to take care of me?" She declares, staring into my apologetic eyes. I know she feels no sorrow for them.

"Goodbye, Dad. Take care," she says, as she rushes past me. Away.

I just stand there, like a dummy. Like a statue. Like me.

"Sir, how long has it been?" the officer asks again, impatiently.

"Eight years," I respond.

"Sir, why don't you go home?" he scoffs.

"Please. She's my only daughter."

"I wouldn't want to come out as pessimistic, however, if she would've wanted to come back... she

would've done it by now," he confesses. "You should simply hope she's still alive."

Rage overtook me like a gust of wind to the head. Knocking me off my feet.

"How dare you! How dare you!" I screech.

"It's only the truth, sir."

"How dare you! How dare you!"

"Go home, sir. And don't come back again." he warns as I get escorted out by a couple of gentlemen in uniform.

I get home, to my lonely hotel. I have kicked out all the guests. I have damaged walls beyond simple repair. All the paintings are sliced in half. What am I even doing with myself?

Why can't she come back? Why?

I feel this empty hole in my heart as it trickles down to my stomach: an empty pit of nothing, punching its way out. As it tortures me, above and beyond. The feeling of being alone forever, of being like this forever. It's more terrifying than death.

I feel my jaw clench, as tears race down my dirty face. How long has it been since I showered? Since I've eaten? Since I've slept? Since I've lived with happiness?

I can't keep feeling like this. This feeling it's so hard to bear. It hits me so hard. I've given the people I love most bits and pieces of me. Entrusting them to never let me go, to never leave me alone. I've given them a gun pointed to my chest, hoping they wouldn't pull the trigger.

They pulled the trigger. Three times.

One after the other.

No warning.

I'm suddenly awake. I'm drenched in puddles of sweat and tears. I look outside the window, and it's dark. It was a pastel, early morning sky, when I first fell asleep.

11:47 pm. Have I been asleep this whole time?

3:00 am. I must have fallen back asleep. This time, however, I am awoken by a call. The same call I've heard twice before: Griffin! Griffin! Griffin!

This time louder and more strident. No matter what kind of heavy sleepers the girls are, in the room above the guys, they must've heard the call. It's still ringing through my head. Like when my grandma would kiss me on the cheek, right by my ear.

I race down to my head set and listen. Apparently they had already started talking.

"Who keeps calling your name?" Pierre groans.

"I'm not sure, but I'm glad to know it wasn't in my dreams. Nightmares are the worst," Griffin responds.

"Where is everyone?" Samuel growls, in his sleepy voice: deep and cranky.

"In their room?" Pierre responds.

"Oh, right," Samuel remembers as he rolls over. "So Pierre, will you please shut up? It's very annoying. 'Griffin Griffin Griffin', shut up, bro."

"It's not me," Pierre announces.

"Then who is it?" Griffin exclaims.

"It's probably Samuel," Pierre snaps.

"Why would I call Griffin in the middle of the night?" he requests, as I hear him flicking his alarm clock, which makes a tick sound. "Or better yet, at 3 am."

"Well, why would *I* call him in the middle of the night, huh?" Pierre exclaims.

"I don't know, you're Pierre," Samuel declares. "Now, let me sleep."

"Stop playing that card," Pierre growls.

"Which card?" Samuel inquires.

"The I'm-so-tired-I-can't-be-bothered-with. We all know it was you," Pierre explains.

"Okay, you know what?" Samuel responds. "Griffin, who called your name?"

"I have no clue. I thought I was dreaming," Griffin says once more.

"Who would call out your name in your dreams?" Samuel smirks, as he chuckles.

"Whose voice did it sound like Griffin?" Pierre sternly inquires.

"I don't know," Griffin responds.

"What do you mean, you don't know? You have to know," Pierre exclaims.

"Stop yelling, you'll wake up the girls upstairs," Griffin announced.

"Sorry, sorry," Pierre apologized.

"Can we just go back to sleep and figure this all out in the morning?" Samuel proposes.

"Yes, I love that idea," Griffin agrees.

"How could I have been so stupid?" Pierre finally says, after a minute or two.

"What?" Griffin and Samuel respond in chorus.

"You two are some sort of allies," Pierre exclaims.

"What in the world are you talking about?" Samuel questions.

"You have one another's back or something. I don't know yet," Pierre grumbles.

"Well, think about it and let us know in the morning," Samuel rasped.

"No," Pierre hisses.

"Hey, Pierre? If I didn't know any better, I'd think *you* are trying to frame *me*." Samuel bellowed. "You never did like me."

"That's it. We will talk about this in the morning, with everyone," Pierre concludes.

"Great idea, mate," Samuel agrees, in his half-asleep tone.

"Goodnight," Pierre shouts and a door bangs open.

"Where are you going?" Griffin questions.

"To sleep," Pierre barks.

"Outside?" Griffin asks, bewildered.

"Yes! In the hallway." Pierre shouts once more.

"Why would you do that?" Griffin implores.

"I don't want to be in a room with murderers," Pierre responds.

"We haven't killed you this whole time and we've certainly had some opportunities. Why would we kill you right now?" Samuel teases, as I hear his chuckles muffled, probably by his pillow.

"Stop joking around and come back to sleep, Pierre," Griffin says.

No answer, instead I hear the door slam shut.

9:30 am. Breakfast. Sausages and bread layered with soft, warm butter. I serve them their plates, fill their cups and leave. To them that's all I am. To myself, I am so much more.

I go to my 'hiding spot' under the dining room stage and wait for conversations and accusations to pile one on top of the other till it all comes crashing down.

"So who called Griffin's name last night?" Pierre demands, as he and Scarlet's arm are crossed.

"What are you talking about?" Renata questions.

"Last night, someone called Griffin's name, three times," Pierre continues nastily, as he sips his coffee.

"Let's not forget the most important fact, at 3 am…" Samuel adds, yawning. Today, his hair isn't fully gelled. Instead, I can pick out some light waves through his hair.

"I'm a heavy sleeper, I heard nothing," Renata adds, as she lifts her reading glasses on her head.

"Well, as I said last night, it wasn't me," Pierre is defensive once more. "If that's what your inferring."

"It wasn't me either though," Samuel exclaims, as he lifts his sweater over his head and places it on the empty chair on his right.

"Is this what you have been doing this entire time?" Leonie inquires, as she looks around the table. "This useless bickering?"

They all look at her, however, nobody answers.

"What are you five years old? This is absurd," She sighs.

"Weeks of this?" She adds, gesturing around the table. She shakes her head in disapproval.

"We're sorry," Pierre responds, just to say something.

"No you're not," Leonie grins, as she rolls her heavy painted eyes. "Now let me think."

Again, nobody said a word. Maybe Leonie is what they need after all.

"Griffin?" Leonie calls. She picks up her slippery hair and ties it back, into a low ponytail which hangs loose on her back.

"Yes?" Griffin answers.

"Do you sleep talk?" Leonie asks.

"No, not that I know of," Griffin responds.

"Okay," Leonie responds, as she scribbles something down on a tissue she had in her purse. "Are you a light sleeper?"

"No, not usually," Griffin says, after a long pause. Was he thinking? Do you have to think whether or not you're a light sleeper?

"Mhm," Leonie moves one. "Samuel…"

"Yes," Samuel exclaims.

"Um," Leonie cocks her right eyebrow. "Are you a light sleeper? Or do you sleep talk, or sleepwalk?"

"No," Samuel negates.

"Mmm, ok," She's not satisfied with the answer.

"Pierre?" Leonie asks. It's like she's questioning different victims in a courtroom.

"You couldn't possibly think it's me?" Pierre exclaims, as Leonie looks at him, annoyed. Her head slightly tilted, her eyes wide.

"I came here to be fair, not to be a good sister," Leonie snaps.

This time it is Pierre who rolls his eyes.

"Pierre?" Leonie repeats.

"What?" Pierre snaps back.

"You are still a light sleeper as always, no?" Leonie questions, as she taps the pencil on the table.

"Yes, ma'am," Pierre teases.

"You better change your attitude. Or I will leave this instant," Leonie warns.

"You wouldn't dare," Pierre laughs.

"Oh," Leonie fake chuckles. "I could leave this instant."

"What's the next question?" Pierre demands changing the topic.

"Have you developed any form of sleep talk?" Leonie carries on.

"No, I have not," Pierre coolly answers.

"Have you heard the call, last night?" Leonie turns her head to face the girls.

"Yes," Scarlet answers.

"Okay, last question," Leonie reveals.

"Does this call happen every night?" She questions.

"Lately it has," Pierre complains.

That, I did not know. I've only heard the call a couple times.

"Always at 3 am?" Leonie requests.

"Yes," they all respond.

"That's so strange…" she carries off.

"Okay, here's the plan," Leonie announces. I listen closely. "Tonight we will all stay up until 3 am."

They all nod in response. Without realizing it, I do the same.

That night, they all fell asleep hours before 3 am. I stayed up. Nonetheless, I didn't hear the call.

I can't sleep. I escape my room, with a growling intention to take a stroll outside. I approach the lobby and grasp the entrance door handle. Smooth, with a green tint where most people have previously grasped the handle. I do the same, as a faint ding sound greets my ear. I stop mid-tracks outside the door and follow the sound.

I find a phone resting on the couch. I tap the screen and a picture pops up. It's Pierre and Scarlet, their backs turned towards me. They are seated on some paintless docks. Their shoes rest by their side. The sunset ahead of them. I turn the phone around, to find Pierre's driving license through his clear phone case. This is Pierre's phone.

Unfortunately, I'm intrigued by the text. I glanced at it, 'by accident'. It reads the following:

Okay?

Under that:

How long till you're done? Come home. Also, you can tell Griffin about the feelings for Scarlet (if you haven't already done so), he knows what to do with the information.

Under that:

Hey

I grip the phone firmly, too firmly in my wrathful hands. I battle the raging urge to throw the phone to the floor. The texts are from a certain Fredrick Junior and there's a smiley, yellow face beside them.

Nobody outside of this hotel knows about poor Allen's death. While so many know about the strong, undeniable feelings Allen had towards Scarlet. Whereas, Allen thought it was only he who knew about his feelings. They were *his* feelings. *His* property. They ripped that away from him. Fredrick planned to use Allen's vulnerability against him, and somehow Griffin is involved in completing this task.

And I'm willing to bet my life that Pierre would've
allowed it.

Chapter ten

A couple of weeks passed. Maybe more. The time passed swiftly but slowly.

Allen's death hasn't been mentioned in days. Maybe a week. I haven't heard any calls at 3 in the morning. Leonie still remains behind the hotel's walls. She has come to the bizarre conclusion that Samuel sleep talks without realizing it. Of course, there's not an ounce of proof. It's the best they can come up with. They are stuck. They can't leave this place, without finding a solution. Until they find a conclusion to this - whatever this is - they stay here. Stuck inside the hotel. And stuck between all the theories, guesses and opinions, which whisper through the night.

Outside, spring has approached our grounds, melting the ice from the sturdy ground, revealing a fresh, dirt path. The perfect breeze and freshly cut grass.

Today, my guests will go swimming in the pond.

"Now, I don't think it's the best idea. The pond will be quite frigid," I warn, but the rest of them are already stripped of their warm clothes. I get goosebumps, just by looking at them in their thin bathing suits.

"Larry, sir. You have to live a little," Leonie laughs. "Plus, it's spring."

"Yes, I know but, it is still explicit that the water is cold," I explain. "I wouldn't enter the water, even if it were summer."

Imagine all the creatures which reside in this lake:
leeches, water snakes, toads, frogs, insects...

Just as my mind hurdles over the images
displayed in my head, Samuel jumps into the pond.
After a couple seconds, he swims back up to the
surface, his wet hair slides down on his cheeks.

"Well?" I question.

"It's amazing," Samuel laughs, as he splashes
Pierre some drops fall upon my hand. Just as I said,
the water is freezing. That frigid banner that wraps
around your head when you swim in the cold. As it
gets tighter and tighter by the second.

The rest of them all jump in, one by one. Except
Scarlet.

"Are you not going in?" I ask her.

"Uh, no," she replies.

Pierre begs her to enter, about five times.

"I'm scared of snakes... in the lake," Scarlet
finally says. Understandable.

"Well, number one, this is a pond," Pierre begins
saying as he splashes water to her feet.

"Still means they have snakes," Scarlet complains
as she backs away.

"No it doesn't, and... they won't do anything to
you anyway," Pierre exclaims.

"If it helps..." I begin saying, "Scarlet..."

"Yes?" she responds, at least she's listening.

"Many of my relatives swam in this pond for
many years and none ever encountered a snake," I
explain.

After some convincing she hops in.

I take a seat on the moldy bench which sits before
the vast pond. I grab my newspaper out of my dark

coat and realize the emptiness in my inner right pocket. I ignore this and manipulate my eyes to read the paper. I cross my ankles and adjust my eyeglass a little under the bridge of my nose. It certainly isn't winter anymore as I feel sweat accumulate on my temple.

It's been hours, that my eyes dance upon the words in front of me, not concentrating on a single one. I look up from my paper and look on top of the water.

A crocodile-green color paints the pond. The idea of starting a diary knocks by my door, but quickly leaves. It's been twenty-three years since Myla left. All that's left to do is... pray that I don't die alone.

I want to get into the water but my fears grasp me by the ankles and pull me to the ground. To the grass. I sit. I look at the clouds. I wait. I wait. For what?

I hear a small splash evoke from the middle of the pond. A slim, round, fruit sprouts to the surface. I get on my elbows to observe it.

The fruit slowly starts to develop into a tall branch, standing vertically on its own.

It's not a fruit, it's not a branch, it's a head. A massive head towering the hotel. It looks like a snake, but there's something elegant about it. It moves with such grace, such divinity. It's daunting.

He has corals spouting from his stomach. A line design tattooed onto his back, in crimson red. A translucent veil-like texture runs down his jaw, pearly white against the dark water. Algae, or rather vines basket his head, like a crown. Like a king.

*Fern green gems adorn his eyes, vivid and bright.
Innocent. With a past.*

*I'm torn between the beauty of this creature and
the majestic size of it. I'm torn between admiring it's
every inch or running to safety.*

*He moves his head in a circular movement and I
look into his illuminating eyes, lightning runs
through my body, touching my every nerve. From the
skin on my rough cheek, to my worn fingertips. A
sense of hope. Who knows maybe, Myla will come
back? Maybe.*

And just like that, the creature leaves.

*I question whether to jump into the lake and look
for him. I'm insane. It's massive, it can crush me in
a split second. Drown me by the minute.*

I leave.

I cowardly left. How foolish. How stupid, I had
been.

I blink my eyes a couple of times till my eyes
adjust to the people in the lake, swimming and
laughing. What if… what if he approaches from the
surface, like he had done years before? What if he
isn't content that visitors are in the pond… his pond?

I decided not to stress over it, especially because I
haven't seen the creature for some time now.

Night falls upon us and my guests go to take a
shower and get ready for dinner.

Overall, I'm extremely happy that they had an
amazing day. Sometimes, I feel like I haven't been
the greatest host. I will try harder. I will.

"Please come out now," I whisper. Wishing, he
shows up tonight. It would give me the much needed

boost. To electrify my body till it's numb, till I'm drugged to elation.

After having seen him, this insane beauty, too great for artificial words. Obnoxious guilt climbs back into my brain at night, and tonight I'm able to block it. To shut it off, once and for all. We all have that miracle which seeks us, never have I known, I was worthy of seeking.

That night I cleaned up, after years of ignoring the chaos living on the floors of the hotel. The mortal glass pieces. The spilled cups of coffee. But it was nothing compared to the catastrophe which lived in my brain, in my memories. Nonetheless, I clean it all. I clean my plate spotless.

He has come back. This time in the moonlight, under her long fingers.

But, Renata is standing there, her hand over her mouth. No. She saw him. As much as I hate to admit it, I am immortally jealous and viciously protective and insanely obsessive. My nerves tick and turn, grow furious that she has seen *my* hope.

Nonetheless, I can't help but admire that he's so beautiful under the moonlight. The designs on his back, now glowing a passionate red in the pitch black sky. His scales shimmering, like millions of miniature mirrors. His soft, sweet expression, identical. His eyes- his eyes are gone. Or rather closed. Shut.

"What are you doing here?" I exclaim, more angrily than intended.

"I- I wanted to ask if I could help to make dinner?" she blunders.

"When have I ever needed help? Tell me?" I snap, as my toes curl inside my shoes.

"Sorry," she stutters. "I'll leave."

I can tell from the tone in her voice that she wants me to ask her to stay.

"It's fine. Just - just stay."

"Okay."

A silent gap.

"What is this?" she asks. As I look at him, at my hope. He is doing his circular motion. Gliding around the pond, just as he pleases.

"It's- I really don't know."

"Whoa," Renata gasps, as she looks at him again.

"Beautiful, I know."

"Does he live in the pond?"

"I'd love to say yes but, I must say, I haven't got a clue," I confess, as she nods in response.

"How many times does he come up?"

"I've only seen him twice," I sigh, as I look at my hope as much as I can. I must take it all in while I can. "This being the second time."

"What a shame," Renata announces, as he re-enters his kingdom. His pond. He's gone.

"What's for dinner?" Leonie approaches us. Has she seen my hope too? "What are you doing here?"

No, she hasn't seen a thing.

"Nothing," I respond. "I'm coming, I'm coming."

We walk back inside, as I go to the kitchen.

Pierre has decided to play for us after dinner. Violin, if I'm not wrong...This should be great...

My mistake, Pierre is singing for us, even worse. He sounds like a dying mouse. It's horrid.

"Alright, that's enough for tonight," I announce as the rest of them thank me with their eyes.

"Aww what a shame," Leonie teases.

"I've improved, you see?" I hear Pierre say to Scarlet, as he puts his arm around her shoulder. She doesn't respond, as Leonie breaks out into a joyful laughter.

"Larry, can we do something?" Renata asks me, as I grab my half-full glass of wine.

"What would you like to do?" I question.

"Can we go to the library?"

"Why, of course," I exclaim.

"What's that?" Pierre questions.

"We are going to the library," I refer to Renata and myself.

"Yes," Griffin cheers. They are coming too; this should be fun.

They follow me to the library like ducklings.

"Here it is," I proclaim.

"Thanks," They respond in chorus.

I debate whether or not to stay with them or step out of the door and listen to what they say, while I am 'gone'. Will Renata tell them about my hope?

I decide to secretly listen. I hide behind the door.

"It's a poem," Pierre declares.

"This time," Samuel announces as I hear his fingers shuffle through the very limited pages.

"What do you mean?" Renata wonders, as I hear her footsteps approach to where I assume Samuel is seated.

"Well, the story, that tale," Samuel slowly explains as Scarlet interrupts him mid-sentence.

"Which was true," she exclaims.

"Can you remind me how it was true?" I hear Pierre ask her, nicely, and politely. What happened to him?

"Yeah," Scarlet responds. "Well, I never got to finish speaking last time, but in the tale, the story which we read from this very book... There was mention of a particular chest with jewelry, diamonds and riches. Except when I found this chest, there was nothing inside it."

"The pirates never found anything either," Samuel reminds her. "Remember the tale?"

Nobody answered her, until Renata spoke at last.

"Yes. I recall it quite well. The pirates had come to this very hotel to find the chest expecting to find wealthy prizes, and inside the chest was bland air."

"Where is the story now? Where are the pages?" someone says, too rapidly to associate the voice with its owner. I hear more and more pages rapidly being turned.

"I have no clue," Griffin responds.

"So where did this come out from?" Pierre asks, as I hear him grasp a paper. Probably the poem.

"I have no clue," Griffin responds once more.

"Can't you simply read it?" Leonie asks, surprisingly impatient.

"Yeah, yeah," Pierre announces, as he clears his voice. "I'll read it.

'I unmask only when the thunder gasps,

When night breaks its eggshell, pouring onto the earth.

Sometimes, I'm from the tallest branch in my backyard,

While I beg to differ, as the sun discovers,

Me.
The friendly faces, the familiar voices,
Still behold their presence of innocence,
Which showers their bodies like a cape.
Sometimes, I'm from late Friday night evenings,
While I remember that isn't,
Me.
Her calloused hands, tending the rose bushes,
As the wind blows them away. Petal after petal.
As she praises the seconds which they stood,
standing,
hand in hand.
Sometimes, I'm from her safe old house,
While now, safe doesn't content,
Me.
The silent hums and unseen stuns,
Unmask yourself to me.'"

"Well that was…"

"What does this mean?" Pierre asks.

"I- I don't know…" Leonie responds. Practically speechless.

I knock on the door as I practically hear their terrified faces.

"Sorry to disturb you but there's some desert," I announce. Of course, there's no dessert but I needed something to get them out of the room.

I hear them scurrying to the door.

As they exit, I hold the door open for them, as I receive few 'Thank you's'. As Pierre passes by me, his eye offers a hint. I look at Pierre's shirt, unsurprisingly a squared surface replaces his once-flowy shirt.

They have stolen the book.

Chapter eleven

The evening flows rapidly down my fingers like water circles a drain. Seconds are demolished by minutes. Minutes are devoured by hours. Hours are finalized by -

I'm back at the cabin, my feet in wool-warm slippers, my fingers embrace a warm mug and my ears covered by headphones.

"It's time for us to restart our hunt," Leonie proclaims as she sits on one of the beds. She pulls out a sort of music box from under the bed.

This camera which I recently installed is really paying off. I can't help but wonder about all the things I might have missed...

They all gather around the bed, some sit on the perimeter and others stay standing. Leonie opens the music box and inside isn't a record player but rather a knife. More specifically *the* knife.

"Well?" Pierre asks her.

"Will you let her think?" Samuel responds, taking the words out of Leonie's mouth. Pierre rolls his eyes.

"Do you all see this?" She inquires as she points her pinky finger towards the blade.

"See what?" Renata asks.

"This," She says, as she moves it close to their eyes.

"What are we looking at?" Pierre questions, the blade centimeters from his face. Leonie runs her finger down the smooth side of the blade.

"There's a slit, like an opening," Leonie proclaims.

"What does that mean?" Renata wonders, as she takes another look at the knife.

I wish this camera would zoom in. I guess this technology has its limits.

"Samuel has your father ever constructed knives that uh, break open?" Leonie requests.

"No, not that I know of," he coolly responds.

"Leo, what do you mean 'break open'?" Scarlet asks her.

"Well this knife seems to open like a pendant," she explains. As she stands up mid-sentence.

"Like this?" Scarlet pulls out a chain from under her V-neck shirt. A pendant, held on by a thin golden chain. Her nails pick at it until it opens and reveals two photos. Or what I think look like two photos.

"Yes, exactly like so," Leonie observes. As she allows her foot to fidget.

"You believe that is the situation with the knife?" Scarlet says in a slight offensive way.

"Yes, let me show you," Leonie responds as she tries to support her claim.

She picks at the blade and passes the knife around the room hoping one of them can crack it open.

It doesn't open.

"It's voice open, we need the passcode for it to unlock," Samuel explains, as he looks at Leonie. Her face falls.

It's been practically hours, as they each take turns saying random words, hoping for the pleasant sound of 'clank'.

"I already said that," Scarlet barks, in frustration.

"I'm sorry. It's two in the morning. Do you think I remember every single word we've said?" Samuel growls.

"Eggnog," Griffin exclaims with a glowing face. Nothing. The knife doesn't budge.

"What does that have to do with…?"

"It's really good, you should try it sometime," Griffin explains, as they all shoot negative looks at him.

I decide to go to sleep, certain they won't achieve much till morning.

In the morning, simply their presence answers my question: they barely slept a second all night. Scarlet's hair is loosely tied in a low bun, several hairs escape down onto her freckled cheeks. Griffin's eyes now covered by a pair of dark, rectangular-framed eyeglasses, (an intelligent attempt to hide his vivid eye bags), which adorn his squared face. Leonie hasn't even come down for breakfast. Samuel's polo is unbuttoned, while Renata looks neat and in order as always. Her long hair is sometimes loose but today is tied in one braid which rests on her back.

"What will it be today?" I question them.

"I don't know, Larry. Whatever," Pierre snaps.

"Coffee?" Scarlet responds.

"Okay, so coffee for Miss Scarlet and whatever for Pierre," I tease. As Pierre looks at me with his laser eyes. I chuckle as I get poker faces from the rest of them. "Too early, got it."

I make my way into the kitchen and turn on the cooktop while I take a couple of ingredients and mix them together.

A warm scent swims throughout the kitchen, filling my nose. A buttery scent of home.

A thought comes through my mind.

Regardless, I let it do just that, cross my mind and evaporate.

I bring them their plates and sit down with them, for the first time.

"So, I heard some talking last night, is everything okay?" I offer, as I sit in the empty chair next to Samuel.

"Yes, Larry, yes," Pierre sighs. How I wish he had learned some manners in his childhood.

"Yes, it's fine, thank you," Renata finally says.

"Alright, well, if you ever need me…" I say.

"We will tell you," Scarlet finishes my sentence.

"Well, I'll be out on the run today, but I'll be back by midnight," I tell them.

"Where are you going?" Pierre asks and I give him a look, as I walk out.

"He's weird, I'm telling you," I hear Pierre say to the others while I close the dining room doors.

The truth is, I'm not going anywhere. Well, I'm going to the basement. To find out for myself, if the chest is real. But it can't be real, it simply can't be. I'd know. Wouldn't I?

Nevertheless, I creep open a little trapdoor under the huge, crimson red entrance rug. It immediately hits me - how in the world would Scarlet know where this trapdoor was, and lift up the rug on her own?

I start to climb down the shaky and extremely
rusty ladder. I've never liked basements. They
remind me too much of all the blood-curling thrillers
I'd read in my teenage years. And they remind me of
all the stories I'd written, for my pure entertainment.
They remind me of graveyards and where trucks
dump out their load of trash. I'd avoid them at all
costs, but this time I cannot. I finally reach the end
of the ladder, and the candle lights flash on, one after
the other, like immortal echoes.

I remember when I first heard of these types of
lights which flash on with electricity and a
movement detector. I had them installed so that
nobody would get frightened when coming down to
the basement.

*I sip my cup of coffee, furious that the
marshmallows have already sunk to the bottom,
forming shipwrecks at the deep end of my mug. This
new book which I am reading: The Great Gatsby, is
simply divine, and absolutely extraordinary.*

*I inhale the words as if they were air and flip
through the pages like my life depends on it.*

*Reading is my addiction. I read about damaged
souls and in one way or another we heal ourselves.
We compare our pasts and I indulge the fact that
their story is worse than mine. Or rather the words
make it seem so. The way the author manipulates the
words like puppets on a string as they form
masterpieces, more complex and more strenuous
than any statue I've ever seen.*

*I place my mug down, and that's when I realize
my neck is aching from looking down at the pages*

for so long. I roll my neck in a circular motion and I hear a crack. But it's not from my neck.

It's from another room. From the basement.

Has Myla come back? Has Myla returned, moneyless and unhappy? I'm willing to welcome her with open arms in unending hugs and cries of joy.

I jump through the trap door, skipping all the steps on the ladder as I fall on my tailbone. It aches to move. I tremble as I stand.

However, I do, I stand. For her. For Myla.

"Myla? Is that you sweetie?" I practically croak.

It's all dark, for I forgot to take a candle stand with me: big mistake.

Nobody answers, so I call out a little louder.

"Myla? Myla?" I yell and, just as I do, I hear the exit door slam shut.

Someone was in here, someone who wasn't her. Myla would've greeted her old man, if she was here. Right? Right.

What do I do now? She's been gone for more than half her life. I've only been with my daughter for one quarter of her life, who knows what she thinks. What she looks like. What she does. What she believes in. What if she's a stranger to me?

The truth is, I installed the lights for her. For Myla. In hope and faith that she might come back to me. To her father.

The basement retains features one would find in a hallway. The motion detector lights enhance the walls on both sides. But there's no perfect carpet on the floor, there's no vivid painting on the walls, no extravagant fresco on the ceiling. It's all monotone.

A gray shade, while some bricks make their appearance here and there, displaying their natural color. A dusty, sandy layering over the floor, I guess one could call the 'carpet' of the place. While this chilly air swims throughout my body. I walk to the end of the basement. I pass by the exit door, it's a cellar door with a white coating which is starting to chip away. I approach the end of the basement, and at my feet there's a chest.

I head back to my cabin after a long day, as I make myself something to drink, or rather my usual: coffee and marshmallows.

I'm still extremely downcast and subdued that my Jesse rots in the heart of the ocean, alone. She had served me fairly for so many years. Maybe, the thing I love most about her was that she never once left me. Never had she abandoned me. Because, I abandoned her first.

I sit down on my chair and put on the headphones. It's foolish how I pass my time, listening to these kids talking.

"I know it. I know it." Leonie shouts. What in the world is going on?

"You do?" Scarlet asks, as her eyes widen.

"Yes, yes," She announces once more, as she rapidly pulls out the box in which the knife resides from under the bed.

Leonie takes the knife in her well-cared for hands and clears her throat.

"Flaming chalice," Leonie proclaims. As she awaits for the knife to open she's so sure of it. Why is she so sure of it?

"Why a flaming chalice?" Pierre requests her.

"It represents truth and freedom," Leonie begins saying as Pierre interrupts her.

"So?"

"It was also an underground symbol and reference in Europe during World War II. Its purpose was for those assisting Jews, Unitarians and others to escape Nazi persecution," Samuel explains.

"Yes, exactly," Leonie indicates.

"But why that symbol?" Samuel questions.

"Allen's ancestors were survivors of the holocaust. I recall having gone to his house a couple of times with Pierre and he had this pictograph in a black frame, displaying a flaming chalice symbol. I suppose it meant a lot to him and to his family."

"So you believe that Allen custom made this knife himself? So that the knife would 'obey' to that specific keyword?" Samuel questions her.

"Yes. I also believe that Allen has always carried a knife around in his pocket," Leonie proposes.

"What makes you think so?" Samuel inquires. You can practically hear the curiosity in his voice.

"Because," she looks around the room, at each and every one of them. "Because, I checked all his pairs of pants and each of them have a right pocket, custom made. A perfect silhouette of that very knife."

"He did have a personal tailor," Scarlet recalls.

"Interesting," Leonie half grins.

"I just always thought it was because he was," Scarlet begins saying, as she starts to bow her head. "Um, because he was oversize."

"He did," Griffin finally speaks out. This time he's wearing a pair of circular eyeglasses, with no frame. "He has always carried a knife around in his pocket."

"Mhm, yes. Do you happen to know why?" Leonie asks him. She's close to grabbing a hold of the answer.

"Yes, because he always wanted to be careful," he responds, vaguely. She didn't receive the answer she wanted.

"Unfortunately, his safety was his doom," Leonie announces.

"This also signifies that whoever killed Allen must've known about the knife he had, in order to use it to kill him," Leonie adds.

Nobody says anything. While all their eyes yell towards Griffin.

"But how did you find the 'magic' word? And why would it open the knife?" Pierre requests.

"I went to the library for half an hour today and I stumbled across the word, flaming chalice, and it made so much sense. Allen's Jewish and you all told me he always cherished truth and freedom so I thought it was perfect but," Leonie explains as she looks down at the knife, unchanged. "Doesn't seem so."

"You see, that's where you're wrong," Samuel answers.

"Huh?" Leonie stares.

"Look at the knife, Leonie," Samuel instructs.

A thick gold stripe slithers across the knife, like a snake. They all stare at it, for long seconds.

"Repeat the word!" Griffin exclaims.

"Okay, okay. Flaming chalice," Leonie repeats.

"You don't have to yell it," Pierre teases.

"Sorry," Leonie automatically apologizes.

"Look," Renata shouts.

The knife is opening. The knife's blade is splitting in half, down the middle, vertically. Just like a pendant.

A sort of antique rigid white scroll falls out from the middle of the knife. One inch thick. Three or four fingers long and a couple of inches wide. The fact that I can simply see it is a miracle, for the camera is slightly blurry and cannot zoom in, or focus on detail.

"Open it," Pierre pleads.

"Okay, okay, calm down. Without me this knife would still be closed shut," Leonie snaps, however, she wraps her fingers around the scroll. It practically crumbles open.

It's extremely lengthy and I think the sides are smooth and curved at the corners.

"What does it say?" Renata wonders from where she is seated.

"It says:

'My body is strong. So is my mind. I'm hoping yours will do the same. I knew my life was on the line. I made this note a night before my killing. To those who have ended my life, I congratulate you. For, if this note is read, you succeeded. The future stabbing which will be injected inside me, is the cause of the shaking of my hands. It rattles my brain like an endless cradle. I don't have more time, or much space on this scroll either. So let me tell you, my friends, how this is going to work: You will

redeem my soul. You will use your complex minds and understand who did this to me.

Here are the clues: use them wisely and use them correctly. For if fallen into the wrong hands, they can cause more harm than good.

Threats and motives against them all:

Griffin: Oh, my dear Griffin. My oldest ally. You, my friend, were in the room as I was killed, (unless my body was moved). You don't listen to music in the shower, as I'm certain you might say. For you find music in the shower distracting towards your reflective thoughts.'

"What? You liar!" Pierre croaks towards Griffin.
"Let me continue," Leonie trembles.

'Samuel: Samuel, Samuel, Samuel. You've always used me for yourself, selfish. You never did truly like me, you always thought I would outsmart you, who knows maybe today is the day?'

I take a look at Samuel and for the first time he's speechless.

'You, Samuel, have given me the knife. Made by your very bloodline, your father, whereas all my blood will drain out of me and will end me forever.

Scarlet: You gorgeous girl. There's something splendid about you that masks your true ego, your attitude and personality which is simply horrid. I love you, forever. However, the feeling, we both know, is not mutual. Rather, the complete opposite.'

"Okay but," Scarlet begins to complain.

"Let me finish," Leonie implores.

'Pierre: You - you are difficult to write about. If you hadn't stolen my angel, I might have even liked you – maybe -
"Stolen?" Pierre rages. "He never had Scarlet."
"I'm not an object, you fool," She punches his arm. Quite lightly, may I add.
"Let me finish," Leonie exclaims, again.

'Pierre, you know I loved Scarlet for as long as I can recall. You are a coward and you are-were frightened I might take her away from you. You've always wanted me gone, now you have your wish.'

"I'm done," Leonie announces as they keep staring at her, waiting for more.
"Oh."
"May I see it?" Samuel inquires.
"Yea, of course," Leonie hands Samuels the scroll.
Samuel glances at it a few times and turns it over.
"There's more:

'I'm entrusting that my last hours were consumed well. My murder/murderers rest in your hands. They must be discovered.'

"Samuel? Can I see it?" Scarlet questions.
"Here," He hands her the scrolls.
I can see Scarlet is starting to tear up.
"Just his handwriting reminds me of so much," she whimpers, as I'm supposing a tear falls down

her cheek. Because Pierre wipes his finger under her eye.

This scroll can potentially lock them all up for either an extremely long time, or forever. One thing, which I might be the only one to have noticed, since they are all overwhelmed: Renata was never mentioned. She's off the hook. She can lock them all up for good.

"Well, now going to the cops is definitely not an option," Leonie sighs as she runs her hand through her hair.

"You were planning to go to the cops?" Pierre pronounces, as he raises his voice a little.

"I mean, maybe?" Leonie stutters.

"You never mentioned that, Leonie," Pierre snaps.

"It slipped my mind?" Leonie lies, as she shrugs her shoulders.

"Whatever, now we definitely cannot say anything, unless we all want to go to jail," Samuel announces, as he exhales deeply.

"Mhm," Renata agrees. She's noticed she's not on Allen's list either. Surely she won't turn them in?

"So what do we do? And how do we proceed?" Samuel implores as he paces around the room.

"Can't we just cover this up and forget about it?" Scarlet offers. She never once thinks before she speaks.

"Are you crazy?" Samuel fake chuckles: he's anxious.

"Samuel, think about it: we all want to go home. Nobody will confess," Scarlet explains, as she pulls her hair into a high ponytail. "It's an endless cycle."

"You are willing to let the killer go loose… just like that?" Samuel exclaims, as he finally stops moving and stares at Scarlet. He then continues pacing.

"Yes. Yes, I am." She answers.

"That's only because you killed him, Scarlet," Samuel cries.

"No, it's because I want to go home," Scarlet responds, her voice cracks, in between words.

"Okay, okay," Pierre proposes. "Why can't we continue this case when we go back home?"

"Yes, but we'd have to confess to Allen's mother," Griffin reminds them.

"She is going to find out one way or another," Samuel speaks hoarsely, more to himself than the others.

"I guess so," Griffin sighs as he looks down at his hands. He's practically shaking and it isn't because of the thin layer of clothing upon his body.

"We are going home?" Scarlet questions as she looks around the room and Pierre gives her a nod. "We are going home."

She's practically in tears, "We are going home!"

"I'll finally see my mom," she sobs. A tear tumbles down her cheek, as I feel one on my cheek do the same.

"We will leave in five days' time," Griffin explains, as he stands up from the end of the bed. "Because we have to leave on a Sunday, it's the rules of this hotel, don't ask me."

"Who cares about the rules? Let's just leave," Scarlet yells, as she starts gathering some things on the floor.

"I'm scared of what that guy can do," Griffin teases but he's serious. And 'that guy' is me.

"Me too, honestly,"

"Fine. We'll leave on Sunday." Scarlet gives in.

"But, Allen, you guys are willing to fail his soul?" Samuel barks.

Nobody responds. They know it's selfish, but they want to go home.

"Leo?" Pierre finally calls, as he shakes her left shoulder.

"Huh?" She's figured it out.

"We are going home," Pierre announces. "We will leave this…"

"We can't," she sighs.

"What? Why not?" Scarlet barges in. Her tears, still fresh on her molded skin, like water to dirt.

"Because of that," Leonie sighs as she points to the bug I installed several weeks ago, on the window sill.

"What is that?" Pierre shouts.

"A recording device: Larry is onto us," Leonie explains, as I feel a need to take a step back. Why do I feel like one of those villains in the movies, where everyone chases after him until he is caught. Nonetheless, it is quite their destiny. Villains are always portrayed as evil. They originated with weapons in their back pockets, which grow into their reputation, as they perish in an empty barred cell.

I don't believe that. Everyone is born equal. Human. The people who they are influenced by shape them into who they become.

"Did you hear me? Larry is onto us," Leonie repeats.

"What?" Griffin streaks.

"He can turn you guys in for good. I could lose my license. My job." Leonie shouts, as she joins Samuel's pacing.

"How long has it been there?" Pierre implores.

"I don't know. Can someone please…" Leonie gasps for air. "Can someone do something?"

"What can we do?" Pier shouts.

"Can you two stop moving? I'm about to throw up!" Scarlet shouts, indicating Samuel and Leonie as she sprints for the bathroom.

I see Renata, her head in her hands, her long bangs covering her face. What is her face dominated by? Is her face filled with frustration? Or rage? Woeful?

"Oh my lord. What if I get kicked out of school?" Griffin hesitates. He stares blindly at the wall.

"Is that what you're worried about? School? We could be in jail for the rest of our lives," Pierre scoffs.

"Someone smash that thing!" Leonie rages as she points to the bug.

"What?" Samuel shouts.

"The bug. That thing," Leonie mumbles. "It can still hear us."

"Okay, okay, just break it with your shoe," Pierre indicates, as Griffin fails in doing so.

"Just throw it in the lake," Pierre insists as Scarlet re-enters the room and returns immediately back to the bathroom.

"Enough," Leonie roars. She grabs the bug, opens the window and throws the bug out of the window, I

assume, and it sinks deep into the lake. I hear a static
noise, through the headphones and now nothing.

They haven't noticed the camera yet, good.

Now I see their mouths move but it's useless, for
they have discovered the bug. I take off the
headphones and march to the hotel.

<u>Chapter twelve</u>

Tonight, as my head lies upon the silky pillow, my eyelids grow heavy upon my eyes. My surrendering legs seem to sink into the mattress, however, my mind screams. So many thoughts are thrown across my mind and they come back and forth like a Newton's cradle. They come crashing towards my mind, disturbing my much desired deep sleep. The urge to shut off, to relax under the feather-like covers. That burning sensation to take a break from all my problems. To sleep. To pause.

Nevertheless, this doesn't happen. I sigh as I stand and wander to my window. I stare out the window. Most of the windows in the hotel are the same: a garden window frame, white and smooth. Nonetheless, the windows here, at the cabins, are all the same: similar to the circular ones found on boats. The ones sailors called portholes, or bull's eye windows. Either way, they are displayed throughout the cabin, in a black frame and in different sizes. The one in my bedroom is a reasonable and honest size. The size of a big pot, which one uses when cooking pasta or rice.

I gape at the night sky and let my thoughts overwhelm me, pleased with the opportunity to admire the beauty of the night without feeling it's frigid air. I continue to observe until my body gives in and allows me to collapse.

It feels like seconds later when I'm awoken by a call. *The* call.

I finally get up from the stool which I had placed beside the window and fallen asleep on. I check the clock: 2:56 am.

"Griffin! Griffin! Griffin!" it croaks three times and stops.

What is this noise? Who keeps calling him? I thought I would only hear the call when I stayed the night at the hotel, apparently not.

I waddle out of my room and into the kitchen where I leave a candle at all times. I grab my single candle stand with an old candle already on it as hardened wax flows down the sides while new, warm wax develops in the center, as I light my candle. I stomp outside, the night is still cold. Chilly, winter's moonlight. I raise the candle stand closer to my weary eyes. In the far distance a dark silhouette of a crow penetrates the moon's rays. He stands on one scrawny leg on top of a fallen tree trunk. I suppose he spots me, for he croaks and flies off. I trudge back up the stairs.

Was it a crow? All this time, calling Griffin's name? Surely he'd have to hear it from somewhere to…

I'm midway climbing the ladder to the loft, where my bed lies, as I hear the call again.

"Griffin, Griffin!"

Oh my days. This time I barely took two steps outside when I found the crow by my rocking chair on the porch. His jet black coat camouflages on the dark ground. His sole raw bone leg keeps him standing sturdily. I take one last look at this bird and I march back upstairs.

"Griffin!"

That's it. I'm going to murder this darn bird. This time I barely get up from my bed before I see a bright yellow eye staring at me from the window. *His* bright yellow eye.

I jolt back in surprise and quickly recollect myself. How did this bird follow me up here?

I'm a tad uncomfortable to approach the window but, I do. As I do, his eye looks abnormally large and a foul yellow color: bright but dark at the same time.

"Shoo! Shoo!" I yelp, as I tap constantly at the glass. He won't budge. He doesn't even dodge the tapping of my finger against the window.

It's just insane to think I have to stay up because of a witless bird that cries 'Griffin' at night. I'm not Griffin, buddy. Go annoy the crap out of him, please.

As I stomp down the stairs and step back outside, I grab a tiny pebble from the surface of the dirt in order to try and get the bird to move away. I rub my eyes as they start to blur and shake my legs as they start to numb. I can barely feel the pebble poking and rolling around in my closed fist. I feel a pain to my head. I'm asleep.

I'm on a thunder cloud, it's a warm shade of purple. I feel the thunder strike me, electrify me, orange. I feel my feet evolve around this airy, light, feathery-textured mass as I glide step after step. The horizon fills with clouds. As I move, I feel my foot stumble and I'm suddenly imbalanced as my body follows my misled foot as I descend down into the dark. I watch the clouds above me get farther away. As I plummet, the downpour starts to drench me, soak me, sink me, until I'm surrounded by the underwater.

I'm re-woken. It's mid-day, because the sun is right above my noggin. No birds chirp. No gentle breeze which persuades me to carry on with the rest of my day.

"Larry? It's after one." Is how I'm greeted as I enter the hotel, past the entrance doors.

"My mistake," I mumble, as I grind my teeth under my thick, coarse skin.

"Well, we wanted to inform you that we are leaving on Sunday morning," Pierre squeaks following me as I race to my reception desk. I give him a look and wonder why they have decided to leave, after having found the bug which I placed in their room.

"I won't be available tomorrow morning," I inform him, as he tries to come with me behind the reception desk, while I point to a couch that will soothe his liking.

"Okay…" he responds as he sits on the couch, tapping his left foot in constant repetition. "When will you be back?" he adds.

"Not for a week," I announce, as I uncap my pen.

"But, we wanted to leave," Pierre exclaims, as I slowly lift my eyes. We exchange stares.

"So?" I request as I guide my eyes back to the paper.

"We want to go home." he repeats, thinking I hadn't heard him initially.

"Leave today," I propose. I close my eyelids, as a plain courtesy to roll my eyes without the result of Pierre's knowing.

"Oh," he squeaks. "But, Griffin said we had to leave on a Sunday?"

"Do you believe all that everyone says?" I respond with another question, as he gets up, and stomps out the room.

"We are leaving today!" he shouts from the room next door, as cheers slowly accompany his words.

"Pierre come back here," I demand.

I hear the sound of his footsteps grow louder.

"Yes?" he asks, annoyed.

"I said you could leave tomorrow," I begin. I lift my eyes to meet his, "But I don't recommend you leave."

His eyes glare at me with shock.

"As soon as you step foot out of here, I'm going to the police," I inform him with a vivid grin on my face.

Still, he's speechless.

"So, either you figure out who killed Allen or you are all stuck in here," I continue. He shivers as I mention Allen's name.

"No," he mumbles. I glare at him with curiosity.

"You can't. If you did turn us in, you'd go in too," he rebuttals.

I sigh.

"I'd risk my couple years in jail, to lock you all up forever," I grunt.

"You see, Larry. I don't think you have it in you," Pierre concludes, as he walks out the room.

"You just wait," I whisper.

In the following hours they prepare their luggage, gather all their loose laundry, eat a late lunch, and finally check out.

"Thank you, for everything," Renata smiles, as I hand her back her passport.

I nod in reply, as I open the heavy entrance doors for my guests, one last pull. The rest of them make their way through the entrance hall for the very last time and out of the doorway forever. I observe them get into Leonie's car. I hear the car's engine turn on. It rumbles down the hotel's entrance path. They merge within the trees.

They are gone.

Now, all that's left for me to do is deliver the truth.

<u>Chapter thirteen (part one)</u>

Her house is far from what I thought it would be. I thought it would be elegant and extravagant, a minimalistic style with a pinch of antique. No, it's a classic square house with a couple of square windows on the sides, the roof consisting of crown brick color roof tiles and a minute garden at the entrance. I suppose that's why my nose is filled with the sweet fragrance and the buzzing of bees is ringing in my ear. Pebbles adorn the passageway leading to the arched wooden door. Standing on the door mat, I press the doorbell as I hear it's distant sound echoing inside the house. Finally, she opens the door, with one hand, as her other one is occupied by a wooden broom. Her wiry hair is tied back into a low bun while her freckled cheeks burn red. She brushes off some of the dust from her apron which covers her blouse and long skirt. Then, her eyes finally greet me.

"Hello, Myla."

"Myla, Myla! Come on, please stop running from me," I gasp, as my lungs try to punch their way out of my chest.

She doesn't answer me as I see her loose hair ride behind her as she maneuvers her way through the crowd.

"Myla!" I shout helplessly as I bump into a mid-aged lady who looks at me with judging eyes and vexed eyebrows. As her eyes finally let loose I lose Myla. I stop abruptly and take a rapid look around. The market seems as if it has expanded in the past

*hour, people of all kinds have made their presence:
a wide age rage: from crying babies all the way to
elderly people with hunched backs, ethnicities of all
kinds. I hear so many diverse languages, many fresh
to my ears. But I cannot let my curiosity lead me, I
cannot lose her, I crawl under a young couple
holding hands and find Myla behind a blacksmith's
stand.*

*I grab her right wrist firmly as she tries to let
loose. She succeeds and once more I find myself
racing after her. I pass food stalls, clothing
purchases, wealthy heirlooms, chickens… as I
finally catch up to her. I grab both her wrists and
pull them behind her back as I dryly exhale on top of
her head.*

"Let me go," she hisses.

"I just want to talk to you," I plead.

*"Help! He's kidnapping me!" she shrieks as
stranger after stranger slaps me across the face, and
once again she escapes my grasp.*

*This time I'll play smart. I will wait in the
shadows until they are all gone. Hoping. Praying
that Myla will still be here.*

*I had come to the market for leisure and that's
when I saw her. When I saw Myla. It was in that
moment that I knew I'd finally found my daughter.
Our eyes locked for a split second and then she was
off again. Running from me and I, chasing her. I
wouldn't let her escape a second time. So here I am,
waiting and praying that she might turn up.*

*There's barely any hungry customers left, let
alone merchants. The sun has surrendered, as the
moon celebrates her victory. The chaos which once*

filled the air: talking, negotiation. Ribbons, banners, flags and stickers. They all rest on the ground, covering the beige of the sand and the brown of the dirt.

I hear her coming at a slow, uneven pace.

She's carrying a basket in her free hand, as her body leans towards the heavy weight, like a magnet as her unbalanced steps stroll down the one-way path.

This is it. I sprint and take her by surprise. I wrap my arms around her and cover her sweaty mouth.

I can feel her heart beat expeditiously as she struggles to be let free. I grab a rope from my back pocket and tie her wrists together. She realizes her next game plan is to please me. So she does. She finally sits. I do the same.

It's only now that I see her, I realize I practically don't know my own daughter. Strands of damp hair strands frame her face, as her hazel almond eyes veer upon me. I now notice a beige cloth which covers her nose and mouth. I continuously try to remind myself that it is my daughter who sits before me. Yet, the more I tell myself, the less believable I find it. I just don't feel all that content, as I dreamed I would be, when I reunited with my daughter. I just feel lost. I feel misunderstood. Why am I wasting this stranger's time?

I approach her as she backs away, hastily.

"Give me some water," she spats, as she speaks, her loosely tied buff falls off the lower half of her face.

"Excuse me?" I implore, as I examine this diamond jewel on her left nostril.

"Please," she requests and I do as she asks. I bring her a cup of water.

"Here," I say, as I bring the cup to her dry lips.

"Okay, that's enough," she replies, as her voice already sounds more smoothing and polished then before.

I look at her once again, she's forty-seven now. Still no gray hairs. None that I can see, anyway. She's all grown up, but under it all, I can still see her. My Myla.

"What?" She inquires, as I observe the vivid tan line which runs across her face, where the buff lay.

"Nothing," I manage to spit out.

"Then what do you want, Larry?" She questions. So she does know it's me. "Yes, I know it's you."

"I- I just wanted to say 'hi'," I propose. I feel so stupid.

"Cut the crap, I haven't seen you since I was eleven. You can't just fix it all up with 'hi'," she exclaims, as she shakes her head in disbelief.

"Yes- yes you're right, sorry," I apologize.

She doesn't respond, keeping her eyes steady on the ground.

We stayed in silence for a few minutes.

"How are you?" I ask her. She glances at me and swiftly looks away.

What did I expect, anyways?

"Is there any way... is there anything I can do to make it up to you?" I beg. I expect no response, once again. She knows I'll set her free anyway.

"Nothing you do or say will make up for what a horrid father you've been ever since mom died." I

know it's the truth, then why is it harder to accept coming from her?

"I know. I'm so sorry, Myla. You can't even imagine the guilt I've lived with... but... but I've changed. I have." She's not convinced.

"I refuse to believe anything that comes from your mouth, Larry."

"I can prove it to you," I mumble in frustration. All I want is for her to give me another chance.

"You're saying you've changed? You're saying you've started to care for others again?"

I gulp back my tears. "Yes. Isn't there something I can do to show you, that I've started caring for others again?"

"There is something actually..." she murmurs.

"Yes, anything, anything," I mumble, practically stumbling upon my own words.

"Well..." she begins, as her voice drops to a whisper. She tells me her wish, as I listen attentively.

"It's a deal," I agree, as I regulate my voice back to normal. The things we are willing to do for the ones we love is absurd, but I've chosen to be absurd. For Myla. To regain her trust. To show her I've changed.

"Good, now untie me, right now," she instructs. I do as she says and we head our separate ways.

Not for long, though.

"I received your postcard, with the address," I say, as my shoes bury themselves in the doormat. She finally nods, an invitation to come inside.

She brings me a cup of steaming tea as I take comfort on her oddly chosen brown sofa'. My feet

tap vigorously on the wooden flooring, as I pick at
my nails. I wait.

The doorbell rings with pride, as I jolt to my feet.
Myla's hand tells me to halt and my body
correspondingly sits back down. I run my fingers
through the few gray hairs left on the top of my head
as she answers the door.

"How can I help you?" she offers, in a high-
pitched tone.

"Mrs. Brown? We'd like to talk to you about your
son," I hear Samuel's voice engage.

"What?" Myla exclaims, bringing sternness to the
matter. She then instantly looks outside, to see if
Allen is hiding somewhere, behind the crowd.

I tramp up behind Myla.

"We meet again," I greet them, as I look upon
them. They all turn to look at me. One by one.
Griffin's quiet, curious stare. Pierre's annoyed
glance. Scarlet's shocked gape. Samuel's sharp
scowl. Except Renata. She isn't here.

Jaws drop, all the way down to the pavement
floor. Their eyebrows raise to the sky, as their eyes
widen to an abnormal size. Their naive brains rotate
and crank as they try and figure out why, why I'm
the one in Mrs. Brown's house?

"Can someone explain what's going on?" Myla
cries, as she notices the connection all of our eyes
have. "And where is my son?"

"Myla, I think they'd like to come in," I explain,
in a serene voice. "Am I right?"

They nod in solemn reply. They follow me into
the humble home, each taking a seat at the wooden

round table. The air starts to smell professional. A formal fragrance.

"So?" Myla implores, her words trickling down her impatient lips.

Samuel clears his throat.

"Mrs. Brown, I hate to be the bearer of bad news but…" Samuel begins, as he takes a pause to look directly into her worried eyes. "Allen is dead."

That's when I could practically hear Myla's heartbeat pump out of her chest, as the bursts of air, from outside, run up my neck. The tiny hairs on the back of my neck strike up in amusement. I watch Myla thrust her body up from her chair as it collapses to the ground in a blast of sound. She manages to anchor her hand to the table before speaking once more.

"My Allen?" Her voice trembles like an eternal earthquake.

"Yes, we are so sorry," Samuel explains. His fakeness begins to bleed out from his words. Although, I know it isn't intentional.

"Are you though?" Myla snaps, as her face reveals an air of disgust.

"Yes, immensely," Samuel responds, in the same lullaby voice.

"Then tell me… *Samuel*," Myla continues, as she emphasizes his name. She turns her hands to fists.

"How did my son die?" She shrieks in pain. At this Samuel seems speechless, after all there are no words to describe it.

"Well, ma'am we haven't figured that out yet," this time it was Leonie who spoke. I look at Leonie

and a little behind her, on the wall in a black frame,
a flaming chalice symbol.

"Who are *you*?" Myla implores, as she points
gruffly to her.

"My name is Leonie, ma'am, I work for the
investigations in the crime department," she holds
out her manicured hand across the table. Myla
rejects it.

"I don't *care* who you are. What are you doing in
my house?" Myla screams, propelling herself up to
her tippy-toes and throwing her palms flat on the
table. As, Scarlet, from across the room, plunges
further back into her seat.

"I'm Pierre's sister, he asked me to help," Leonie
continues.

"He asked you to help? He asked you to help?"
Myla cries in disbelief. "Help you with what?"

"With the investigation, as regards to who
murdered your son," Leonie explains, in a slow,
steady voice. Myla gasps at the last words of the
sentence.

"Murder?" she wails. She falls to the floor into a
ball, her face buried in her legs.

"Yes, ma'am, allow me to explain, if you will,"

"So how long have you known my son was dead?
A day, two…" She gasps. "A week? And nobody
informed me?" Tears invade her eyes as the bullets
rocket from her mouth. She lived that time, in pure
joy, knowing her son was on vacation with his
friends. Oh, how wrong was she.

Myla whimpers as she shrieks, as we all become
blurry.

"How long? How long has it been since he died?" Myla wails. "Answer the question! Please?" She implores, as she re-stands.

"Mrs. Brown…" Leonie begins. Leonie struggles to keep the knot in her throat from rising.

"Tell me," Myla screeches.

"Almost two and a half months," she finally confesses.

I turn my eyes to Myla, her wide shoulders rocking repeatedly back and forth, a boat in the secret ocean.

The air in the room hisses, as the sun outside seems to mirror the expression. She places her fingers on her temple and massages it a tad, her hands then slide into her obscure hair. She purses her lips, snot rumbling down her nose. Then she looks up. I pray for Leonie. Because, Myla's stare took my soul and it wasn't even directed towards me.

"Then tell me… *detective*! Who killed my son?"

"We still have to figure that out," Leonie gasps as Myla breaks into another tsunami of screams.

"But - but, we have quite a few leads," Leonie adds, intending to placate her.

"Is that supposed to console me?"

"No, no, of course not. I know how much this will affect you and I can assure you I will find his killer, if it's the last thing I do," Leonie pledges.

She doesn't respond.

"Mrs. Brown, why don't I come back tomorrow? You must rest," Leonie proposes, as she slides a paper with a number on it towards her. I suppose it's hers.

She doesn't respond.

Leonie starts to get up as I tell her to sit back down and lock the door.

"Okay, then I guess I'll start with who the suspects are," Leonie initiates, her frightened eyes attempting to part ways with mine but failing repeatedly to do so. "Can you please leave the room?"

She's talking to Scarlet, Pierre, Griffin, and Samuel. They nod synchronized.

"No. They can stay," I announce.

"Larry, that's unprofessional. I simply refuse," she complains, her teeth grinding rapidly.

"You've shared your thoughts with them all throughout these months, I'm sure you can do the same today," I exclaim.

"Fine I will. But for future references, it is against the law to place a bug in someone's room," she exclaims, alarmed.

"Oh, I'm sorry, I understand. So… kind of like how you're working for free, being the sister of one of the suspects is against the law," I riposte. "Right?"

Leonie stares at me. Her eyes in shock. She's afraid. Afraid of what I might do.

"Mrs. Brown, we have four suspects at the moment: Samuel Carter, Pierre Andre', Griffin Paddock and Scarlet Smith," Leonie ignores me as her breathing quickens. "I will start with Samuel Carter,"

Then she starts laughing, hysterically.

"Mrs. Brown?" Leonie implores, in a worried tone. "Would you like a cup of water?"

Myla continues to laugh.

"Myla… stop it," I instruct, the rest of them stare at me. I know what they are thinking: how dare I tell a son-less, single mother what to do.

"Myla, that's enough," I shout, standing up, violently sliding my chair against the wall.

"I'm - sorry, this-" she says in between gasps. Then she resumes her hysterical, insane laughter.

I then thrust my chair towards the wall.

"For heaven's sake," I shout. My chair shattered to pieces clearly doesn't grasp her attention. She won't stop laughing. "Allen come here."

In tall, confident steps, Allen marches out of the kitchen, one foot after the other.

"Allen!" Scarlet hollers, as she falls to her knees.

"Allow me to explain," Allen speaks as Scarlet runs to embrace him.

His words rest upon the air, waiting for another phrase to follow. Nobody. Nothing. They rest in shock, their eyes focused on Allen, checking if it's really him. If he has a dimple, on his right cheek, a birthmark on his left arm, dark prominent eyebrows and obscure, almond eyes.

For five to ten minutes all is silent. Scarlet keeps on poking Allen to make sure he's not a ghost and then punching him in the face for making her think he was dead, and then hugging him for minutes, until Allen tells her to get off him. Griffin and Samuel remain so shocked they keep asking each other if they can see Allen too or if it's a dream. They assure each other that dreaming isn't the case and they remain in this statue-like shape. Leonie, on the other hand continues to gasp and scribble on her notepad.

"Would you like me to explain?" Allen asks again. Scarlet pleads anxiously for him to begin.

"This is my grandfather; his name is Lawrence..." Allen points to Larry.

"*The* Lawrence?" Samuel shouts in awe. "Larry is Lawrence? What?"

"Yes, he's the very one," Allen reassures him, Samuel keeps rubbing his eyes: he still thinks he's dreaming.

"What do you mean, *the* Lawrence?" I implore, as I stare at Griffin who seems to be in the same state as Samuel.

"Well, long story, grandpa. I simply told them about some of your childhood stories," Allen answers... I decided to leave it at that for once.

"Enough with the small talk. Can someone please explain to me what is going on?" Scarlet gasps, her mascara runs fresh down her burning cheeks. Real life starts to kick in. They finally realize it isn't a dream, it isn't a joke. Allen is alive.

"I..." I begin as Allen silences me. I nod in reply. He wants to explain it all and he is right, he should explain it, after all it's his story.

"Scarlet, Samuel, Griffin, and Pierre. Less than three months ago, you thought I had vanished from this world; died. But, obviously, that isn't true," He begins. Why does this sound like a speech? He has practiced it.

"Yeah," Pierre scoffs. Of course they are mad. Who wouldn't be?

"I know you're mad," Allen begins, as Pier cuts him off.

"Of course we are mad, Allen. We thought you had passed away, man," Pier shouts, he tries to keep his voice strong but he's on a thin line to tears.

"Yes but-but please if anything, I was the one clouded with anger every single day," Allen resumes, staring at them. "As you know, I have only known my grandpa for about eight or nine months now. My grandpa and my mother met at the town market, they caught up and, well, when mom came home for dinner, she said I'd meet my grandpa really soon."

At the market my grandpa made a deal to my mother or rather to me. Now, before I continue, please believe me, I'm not selfish, I'm not a bad person. I-I simply have a broken soul. So I beg forgiveness in advance."

They all gape furiously at him, in wonder for what sort of 'deal' they had been victims of. Scarlet the only one with pity in her eyes. The rest of them, now, have a hunger for revenge, dominating their eyes.

"I wanted you all to feel the pain I have been going through. The flesh tearing pain. I put you under my misery, so that I wouldn't have to suffer alone. I wanted…"

"What? What did you want- revenge?" Samuel roars, his voice scratching the paint walls.

"Yes. Although you, Scarlet, Griffin and Pierre haven't killed me physically," Allen began saying, as little ponds start flowering in his sorrow-lit eyes, he continues, keeping his voice steady. As steady as he could be.

"You manipulated me, Scarlet. You used me," Allen professes, staring at Scarlet, her hair all over the place. Her once cheery eyes, puffy and red, her forehead boils with sweat, with trauma.

"You. You? You made sure everyone, but I- knew the truth," Allen continues, as he addresses Pierre, who can't help but look away. An air of ridicule in his face.

"You were hiding when I was finally the one seeking. The one seeking help." Allen declares, as he glances at Samuel from the side of his eye. Samuel shows no response. He looks at his feet. Like a puppy being scolded. "You only cared for yourself."

"You- you, Griffin, you tore me apart," Allen finally cries. Screams. Pain. Waterfalls cascading down his strong rocky cheeks. Allen still stands tall.

"Allen! I'm sorry, I really am. Can't we put that all behind us now?" Griffin pleads, as Allen takes no effort to listen.

"You tore me apart, Griffin," Allen wails, as he gasps recklessly for air.

"But- Allen? How dare you! How dare you put me - us through all this misery?" Scarlet ululates, as she steps back from the crowd, her back rubbing against the wall, as she slid down to the floor. Her hands encasing her knees, as she breaks out in a long cry.

"Allen I don't care. I don't care about all your mentality behind it all. Your little play- I want to know how you made us all suffer relentlessly? Right now!" Pierre demands, as Scarlet hollers in the background.

"This goes back to the deal my mother and my grandpa made. I wanted to see if any of you would care if I was gone. Gone forever," Allen explains, his arms tense by his sides. Samuel now catapults from his seat.

"Please, Sam?" Allen begs him, as I block him mid-path to Allen. "Allow me to explain?"

"You've been saying that the whole time, and n-nothing of sense has come out of your m-mouth," Scarlet sobs. While Pierre glares at Allen: an indication to carry on.

"Well, for most of my life, I've thought my only family was my mother. Little did I know that I had such a vast family. Ophelia is Lawrence's grandma-not by blood, she passed away from an old disease, as well as Lawrence's wife, Thalia," Allen explains, as he grabs a paper pad from the kitchen counter and a pencil from the drawer. "Thalia had three children with her first partner; Adelaide, Theo, and Magnus. She had her last child with Lawrence, Myla - my mother. My mother was the youngest. Theo and Magnus, twins, left early at the age of 17, to join the army. While, Adelaide, being the oldest, married at a very young age, around fifteen, and left for Russia with her husband, Kirill. She lives there now."

Allen starts to write some names down on the pad and connect them. The rest of them gather back to the table to observe.

"The twins never married. Magnus died at a young age, when the hotel was under attack. Theo lives less than an hour away from here with his two cats. I know this doesn't amuse you in any way."

"Yeah, it really doesn't. Get to the point, or I'm leaving," Samuel shouts, as Pierre nods in agreement. "I've had enough of this nonsense."

"Theo, he helped me make the crow," Allen spits out, in a haste.

"The crow?" Samuel questions.

"Yes," Allen acknowledges. This was a surprise to me too. "Croaked Griffin three times every so often. It's all coding and fake feathers."

"The one you blamed on me," Samuel roars at Pierre. "You accused me of murder, instead of the fake bird!"

Samuel snickers in absurdity.

"Samuel, Samuel… I'm not the bad guy here," Pierre hisses, glancing at Allen. I can practically feel Allen's unheard injustice rattle upon the table.

"But why?" Scarlet croaks, pouring another cup of water down her throat.

"To get you all against one another," Allen sighs. "I wanted to see if you would fight for me, fight for my justice."

"So, you framed us all? We were part of a 'test'?" Scarlet blasts.

"Yes," Allen responds without hesitation. "I knew Sam would be blamed by Pierre or better, Scarlet would be."

"Like the knife," Samuel snarls.

"Yes," Allen snaps. "Theo helped me design that knife as well."

"While Adelaide, she was in the kitchen the whole time. Cooking and cleaning, for you?"

"Oh my bad, I forgot to say thank you," Pierre chaffs.

"Allen, this is insane. Even for you," Griffin gasps.

Leonie, on the other hand, stays steady in her seat, scribbling note after note. The once- yellow paper has become mostly gray.

"And Arthur, Ophelia's lover, had two brothers, Victor and Louis. Victor died in the destruction of the hotel when it was ambushed by the purple team - long story. And Louis, he's been sneaking into your hotel room when you were out and checking that the bug was still functioning. He's the one who put the camera in the room as well, not Lawrence-"

"There was a camera too?"

"Hold up. In my defense, I put the bug in a pretty obvious spot so that you could eventually find it," I acknowledge.

"Why?" Leonie pries, flipping her three paged journal, in a rush.

"So that you would know I was onto you, and your little plans," I respond. "So that you would believe this. All of it."

Now it was I who was the magnet of stares.

"So let me get this straight, a numerous amount of people were into this 'prank' of yours?" Pierre urges, as I watch Samuel pace around his chair.

"Yes, exactly," Allen responds, his previous tears starting to wilt.

"But... How? How did you fool us so well?" Scarlet stutters, as she finally discovers the force in her legs, propelling her to stand.

"My question is - were you alive on the floor the whole time?" Samuel implores, as his mastermind starts to refunction.

"Of course not," Allen replies. Samuel gapes at Allen: he isn't satisfied with the answer.

"That was an old mannequin from the attic of the hotel, some prosthetics and make up" Allen adds.

"This is just too much," Pierre shouts, as he removes his sweatshirt, highlighting the sweat marks on his pastel blue shirt. "It's insanity."

Scarlet keeps on wailing, and screaming.

"Hey Scarlet, stop. Stop it now," Samuel demands, as she whimpers. "It's not your fault okay?"

"But why Allen? I just can't get it through my head, I can't..." Scarlet shouts.

"I know, it's a lot to take in for one night, why don't we eat something?" Allen proposes, as he indicates towards the kitchen. He stops and adds, "I'm just not perfect."

"How could you? How can you let this go so easily? Oh, Allen, you should go to prison for the rest of your life," Scarlet hyperventilates.

"Scarlet, Scarlet, stop. You'll hurt your voice, let's go grab some water?" Leonie asks her, as she wraps her in a hug.

"No! I don't want water. I want him gone." Scarlet screeches, as Allen starts approaching her. Frightened, she takes three steps back.

"But I forgive you. I forgive you all. Even if saying sorry is mainly easier than forgiving. I forgive you." Allen proclaims, as he takes multiple gasps before he speaks. They all look at him with a shocked expression.

Samuel runs out. The front door bangs against the frame as Samuel scuttles out in a hurry. In the blink of an eye, Pierre's strong scent of cologne flows through the door as well, the door swings open once more and shuts again in a bang, as Scarlet leaves too. The rest of us follow. I grasp the handle, it takes my full arm muscle to get the door to open, for it feels as if we've been snowed in. Nevertheless, once I open the door, a howling gust of wind wraps my face, as a sandy texture grinds my bare forearms. I find myself coughing instantly.

It's a dust storm.

"Samuel! Samuel!" Scarlet's sprinting now.

"Samuel, come back. There's a dust storm," she shrieks.

I see Allen running towards Samuel, his silhouette skitters along the parched meadow.

The wind's howl hisses through my ears, as I feel a sort of adrenaline rush through my veins. I watch as Allen and Scarlet helplessly try and capture Samuel, who gets closer and closer to the heart of the swirl. Pierre, on the other hand, has already turned back around.

"For the love of God," I cry. I march vigorously to the barn, yards away from the house. I hear Myla calling my name, crying for me to come inside. I ignore it.

"I'll go. Come back inside," Myla warns but I allow her words to fly past me along with the current of the wind. My glasses fall off my face to God knows where. My clothes begin to stick to the side of me, as if they were wet. My eyes start burning and itching from all the sand and dust they have accumulated. I breathe in, as grainy air runs up my nose. But I ignore it. All.

Inside the barn, the chaotic wind and sand doesn't reach me. The pure air is refreshing, but I can't lose time. I briskly manage to reach Buck. I hop onto his bare, sturdy back, give him a kick to the ribs and we gallop out. We ride past the unstable barn doors as we bolt through the wind. Under the weeping sun. Between the fiery dirt, rising up, rising up on us.

It's been too many years since I'd last ridden and the stripping of my youth, doesn't help either. Nonetheless, with difficulty I manage to remain on Buck's back.

I try to keep my eyes open but it's impossible. More and more sand invades my eyes, till they rebel to remain shut. The same feeling, as when I get soap in my eyes. I feel sand caress my skin, like an old lady with long, spiky nails. Nonetheless, my legs press firmly to the side of the horse, I will not fail.

I manage to reach Allen and I tell him to go back home. He's skeptical but he agrees once he sees I'm on horseback. I then reach Scarlet. Stubborn Scarlet.

"Scarlet stop. Please. Come back inside, I'll take care of this," I command, as a handful of sand enters my mouth. "Trust me."

"Y-You! You- want *me* to trust *you*?" She pants as the dust and the dirt swirls from the ground under her feet, completely erasing them from my view.

"Then hop on," I panic. I'm stressing, watching Samuel wander closer and closer to death.

Scarlet ignores my request and keeps on racing.

"Scarlet, Scarlet!" I bellow. If I fail in saving Samuel, I wouldn't manage to live with the guilt.

She finally stops running and looks at me, her hair
swirling through the wind on top of her head. She
opens her mouth to argue.

"Well, give me a hand," she shouts, coughing. I
do as I'm told and hold out my hand. She takes it
and hops onto Buck.

I hear her coughing continuously. I hand her a
tissue from my pocket, she snatches it and covers her
mouth.

It will all be worth it because, the farther we get
from home, the closer we get to Samuel… but the
deeper we dive, the closer we are to the heart of the
storm.

"Samuel, Samuel!" I shout. "Stop running."

Obviously he can't hear me, obviously I'm simply
hurting my voice for no reason. I can't bear it; I have
to give it my all. I need to…

There's something I can do.

"Scarlet, listen to me. Listen?" I implore, but she
won't answer. "Listen!"

"Scarlet?" I repeat but again she doesn't answer.
She can't hear me. We are in too deep. I know what
I need to do.

I forget my surroundings, take a deep inhale and
sand fills my nose, I push myself off the horse. I see
Scarlet's shocked expression, her scream silenced,
covered by the guilty whipping of the wind.
Immediately, Buck speeds up, seeing as my weight
has vanished from his back.

I nosedive straight into the ground, my left side,
will certainly be getting bruises. I place my hand
over my hip bone, as it aches, relentlessly. Sinking
my teeth into my bottom lip, to stop myself from

crying, I suddenly feel blood greet my tongue. I realize I bit my lip too harshly. My right hand, which now rests on the left side of my head, trembles and my head feels as though someone sliced a sword into it.

It's fine. I'm okay.

Scarlet's only minutes away from Samuel. In another world, the smart thing to do would be to go home, leave Scarlet to it. Care for my wounds. I don't want to die out here. I can leave. But not today, today I decided to wait. I'm on my stomach, flat on the floor, squinting to see whether Scarlet has succeeded. Or not. Sand enters from the collar of my polo as it flaps, back and forth, against my back.

My head keeps on throbbing. My lip keeps on bleeding. My mind keeps on spinning.

She did it. She did it! Samuel and Scarlet are on Buck's back, riding back towards me: a sign to get up and run home. Go! Go! Go!

But I stay glued to the ground. I feel this inner urge to make sure they come back, that they won't get unexpectedly sucked in by the sand. That they will be okay.

Another part of me, questions, what can I do, or rather, what would I do, if they were to get sucked in by the dust storm? But I wait. I wait.

Until, we all get home safely.

<u>Chapter thirteen (part two)</u>

I find myself home again, in my home. In the hotel's ballroom along with at least half a hundred people. The room's warm lights contrast against the cold sky. The stars are fairly distributed and sparkle almost as bright as the gleaming smiles in the room.

It's been over five or six months since the encounter at Allen's home, bringing us to a late autumn gust. After long weeks of bitterness and remorse, Allen and his friends decided that they all were all going to restart their friendship. A new, clean slate. Because, when you love someone so much, all their flaws, all their sins, all their strange imperfections are so insanely perfect to you.

"Scarlet!" Allen gleams, as he holds out his arms to embrace her. "You look beautiful."

"Thank you," she replies, as she twirls in her cascading, velvety, vermillion dress. Her hair in tight curls, ever so golden under the lights. Her eyes shine with joy.

"Thanks for having me," she adds as she glances at me and mirrors my welcoming grin.

"How have you been?" she questions.

"Very well," I respond. And I'm not lying. Ever since *that* day. The day in which all of the truth was told, or at least most of it. I've been the old me. Maybe it's the new me.

Anyway, I started cleaning up the hotel for a third reopening. I decided to only keep the hotel open during the summer and winter vacations in order to rest and spend more time with family all year round.

It was only last week, that I decided to look for some new employees. So, I traveled a tad. Here and there, only to lead me back to the very beginning. Allen. He offered to help run the hotel with me, on the days in which he isn't in school. These days' coordinate seamlessly to the days the hotel will be open, so it's sort of perfect, in some ways.

"Is Renata coming?" I ask, as I recall not having seen her since their hotel's visit. Whoa, it feels like a lifetime ago.

"Who?" Scarlet asks, as Allen hands her a glass of champagne.

"Renata," I repeat, a little louder, thinking the violin overpowers my words.

"Renata?" she questions. "Who is that?"

"Renata. The one you shared a room with, here at the hotel," I chuckle, how could she have forgotten her friend already? Is she that shallow?

"Lawrence, I never shared the room with anyone but myself," she responds, her eyes serious, maybe a little too serious. "And Leonie but only after she arrived."

"Oh come on. How could you have forgotten? Renata? Slim, brown, puffy hair, was always reading. Freckles and dark eyes." I describe her. Surely, they weren't close but forgetting her already is a little extreme.

"Grandpa? I never had a friend named Renata or anyone with that description for that matter," Allen steps in. He looks at me worried.

"Lawrence would you like a glass of champagne?" Scarlet offers, disturbed, as she tries to change the subject.

"No. No, thank you. I'm - I'm going to use the washroom," I explain, bursting through the crowd. Just as I'm at the very heart of the crowd I encounter Arthur talking to his brother, Louis. Something about gardens. But I pretend not to have seen him. Or heard him when he calls my name.

Once I enter the washroom, I close the door shut and tamper at the lock until I finally hear it clank fasten. How could Renata not exist? I've seen her every day for more than two months. Who saved me when I was drowning in the ocean? When Jesse ran off the cliff into the endless waters? Who was reading those advanced books, day after day?

That's when it hit me. Just like that.

"Finally, you figured it out," Renata friendly chuckles, sitting cross legged on the armchair near the sink.

"Never knew you were like this when you were young, Thalia," I respond.

"Well, what can I say? Youth leaves you at one point or another," she sighs.

"Oh no, Thalia, elegance always seemed to stick by you like a cranky old clam," I scoff teasingly. "What I mean is, I never knew you liked to read so much."

"And yet, I never once saw you step foot in the library," I add, recalling the times we had spent together.

"A temporary hobby," she explains, plainly.

"Sure seemed like you loved it a lot," I remark. "What happened, Thalia? Why did you stop reading, if you loved it so much?"

"I was addicted, Lawrence. Addicted to the fact that every book was going to be better than what life had planned for me," she sighs and a tear flows down her cheek, it vanishes once it touches the floor.

"I was trying to picture myself in the lives of those in the books, I compared those eventful lives to my vanilla life. Even the bad moments which occurred in books seemed to be better than the happiest of my days. Those bad moments in books offered amazing stories and I couldn't help but wish for something -anything to occur. A something exciting. Until, I realized how ungrateful I was. I was consumed with lack of appreciation. I felt pity for myself for no reason. It was an addiction," she explains quickly growing older, years flying by in seconds. Her confession advances her maturity.

I now stare at her, her older self. Her early forties self. She's standing so confidently, so tall. A safe lighthouse while a vast sea of emotions pours from her mouth.

"Thalia, thank you for saving me," I finally say.

"Which time?" she questions, smirking.

"Well, always, really," I answer. "But specifically when I was drowning."

"Lawrence, you did that one your own," and as the last word harmonizes out her mouth, she's gone.

I head back to the party, meeting Myla on the way. She's dressed in a glamorous, rich green, which compliments her eyes. Her mid-length, thick hair, blankets her bare shoulders. While, her right hand rests on the gentlemen by her side, her other hand occupied by a petite handbag.

"Lawrence… Lawrence!" She stops me, mid track.

"Yes?" I glare at her and then glance at the gentlemen beside her.

"This is James... James Fredrick," she explains. "Allen's father."

I look him up and down. From his pitch dark hair, along with his pale skin, all the way to his polished shoes.

"It's a pleasure to meet you," he greets me, and holds out his hand. Wish I could say the same.

"Where were you?" I implore.

"I beg your pardon?" he responds, retrieving his hand back.

"When Allen was growing up, where were you?" I repeat.

"Lawrence, you hardly have the right to ask such question," Myla scoffs, judging me with her eyes.

"For your information, I was looking for you all my life," I respond, in a matter-of-fact kind of way.

But I feel guilty to ruin such a good night. So I let it go. Just for tonight.

"I'm sorry," I apologize. "I'm sorry, can we just have a good time tonight?" I ask, as she nods in agreement.

"I was working as an FBI agent in South America," James intrudes. "It was nice to meet you, Lawrence."

He nods his head as a sign for me to get going.

I skip ahead, only because of the repetitive craving in my throat. I'm yearning for another glass of wine.

"Lawrence! Everything alright?" It's Scarlet.

"Oh yes, it was the wine," I lie. I wasn't about to explain to Scarlet that I'd been hallucinating my dead wife, as a twenty-year old, the whole time.

"Don't drink too much, sir," Scarlet responds as I see Pierre making his way towards us.

"Lawrence! How are you?" he squeaks. After his several week trip to France, his accent seems to be getting thicker.

"Bon," I tease.

"Oh monsieur! Are you saying my accent has got worse?" he chuckles, extra-rolling his r's, purposely.

"Seems like I've found the party," Samuel makes his appearance in a black suit and an unevenly placed bowtie.

"Glad you could make it," I respond as I watch him hug Scarlet. "What a turn of events, huh?"

Scarlet giggles in response.

"Guess so."

"Look who it is," Allen heaps in applause, eyeing Griffin.

"Oh stop it, bro!" Griffin's deep voice flows into the room. Along with his navy blue suit, and his bright red tie.

"You look great, Griffin," Scarlet welcomes him as she tries uselessly to fix Samuel's bowtie.

That's when I notice.

"Scarlet, could you help me hand out some appetizers?" I ask, indicating towards the kitchen.

"Yes, of course," she willingly accepts. "I'll be right back."

Once we arrive in the kitchen, I hand her a silver tray filled with appetizers.

"Where did you get those earrings?" I request,
trying to keep it casual. Although this conversation
will be beyond casual.

"Ugh, I should've known better, than to think you
wouldn't have noticed," she sighs.

"Yeah…"

"Allen and I had just become friends and he told
me about your hotel. My family and I - we were in a
financial crisis at the time. I immediately thought
that this hotel, being filled with riches and such,
could enable me to steal something precious in order
to help my parents out. When I entered through the
basement, through the cellar door, I found the chest,
the same one in those tales we read back at the hotel.
There was nothing in there except these earrings. I
wanted to look for something more but then I heard
you come in yelling your daughter's name. So I only
took these earrings and left," she confesses, pointing
to the earrings.

I growl. All this time, I thought it had been Myla
looking for me, oh how wrong have I been? Wasting
my time, is what it was.

"I'm sorry. I really am. Especially because my
parents didn't accept the theft and made me work
even harder to find a better-paying job. I really am
sorry," she apologizes, taking off the earrings and
handing them to me. The green earrings.

"Thank you," I reply, and I carry them in my
hands. I immediately strode off as she rambled
around. I hear her in the other room offering some
appetizers to the crowd.

"Wait, Lawrence before you go," she exclaims,
jogging back towards me. "You were a good writer,

almost had me tricked with all those make-believe tales and poems. Sorry to have read your personal writings."

I chuckle in response. She knew all along about my early teenage tales about the hotel. The poems, the stories. She knew all along. Why did she play it blindly?

I decide to take the earrings back into the basement inside the chest where they belong.

As I go down the stairs, the temperature lowers with every step I take. As I approach the basement the lights which I had installed flick on, illuminating the area as I approach the chest.

Somehow the silver of the frame still seems to portray its power. Whereas the once navy blue coating has chipped away, revealing the dark wood underneath. The lock is shattered. Scarlet previously broke it in order to open the chest, not having the proper key.

As I jiggle the two earrings around in my palm, I bend down to my knees and open the chest. Obviously there is nothing inside other than dust and insects.

As I place down the earrings in the bottom of the chest, carefully. I see some tiny insects scattering away from where I placed the jewels. And, as I'm about to close the lid, I take one last look at the earrings. Fern green gems.

How are they familiar? I know they are linked to me. But how? Now that I think about it, I'd never actually seen them in this chest. But I could bet my highest possession, I'd seen them before. Where?

I sit there beside the earrings, cross-legged on the frigid floor, as my mind pours out in front of me, awaiting for the connection to light up. Awaiting for that g a s p, where I remember it all.

It's after twenty minutes or so before a thought comes to mind. I know where I'd seen these before. The creature. The pond snake. The one with eyes, so precious, so fascinating, so fern green… My hope.

I pick up the earrings again and skip back up the stairs to the ballroom, filled with chatter and laughter.

"Arthur?" I call out. Roaming through the crowd until I find the particular face I'm calling out to.

"Arthur?" I repeat, until I finally find him, in his wheelchair next to a little bar table.

"Hello, son," he gleams. "Would you like to join me? It's only apple cider."

"Oh no, thank you," I quickly respond. "Arthur, do you recall these earrings?"

He grabs his eyeglasses from his front pocket and places them on his arched nose. I hand the earrings into his puffy hands and watch as he examines them, carefully.

After a couple minutes or so, I question him: "Well?"

"Well hold on some. It's been ninety years I've been alive and you son, are asking my tired old mind to remember a pair of microscopic earrings?" he snaps.

"Sorry," I mumble, as he continues to explore the earrings. Then he hands them back to me. "Well?"

"Yes," he answers.

"Yes? Yes what?" I request.

"Yes, I recall those earrings," he responds. "I gave them to Ophelia, as a gift, a week after our wedding."

I smile and slowly close my eyes.

"Thanks, Arthur," I cheer, as I head over to the window sill. I look out. I look out to her.

"Thanks Grandma, for looking over me all this time," I whisper as joy overflows through my every nerve. Gratitude and appreciation follow not long behind.

Chapter fourteen

Yes. Yes, I wanted the story to end at this but, on the contrary, my story has just begun. The very last two people (Allen and Myla), have left the party and I'm the only person in the room but, I'm not alone. For once, I'm standing solitary in this room and I feel loved. It's just like this exciting and safe feeling in my mind that reminds me I'm not lone in this world. That not everyone is a stranger. That I live for someone.

The sun has started to rise, heating my sensitive heart. I can feel the warmth of its rays across the window sill, which is strange but I like it. Some birds glide upon the horizon, in a V-formation. Which reminds me, it's time to get going.

I bring the empty platters into the kitchen to clean them. Afterwards, I gather the party decorations, store them in a container and bring them up to the attic. I try to hurry the best I can, for I'm supposed to have brunch with Allen and Myla at their house. I simply can't wait. I've always dreamed of relaxing days with my loved ones. Myla even told me that she left a spare car in the garage, in order for me to join them once I had finished cleaning.

I finally exit the hotel's doors and lock up the place. I juggle the key in my hand and think to myself how crazy it is that I put all my safety and trust into this small key, that has to ensure protection for weeks, months, till my return.

I arrive at the garage and, just as I enter, I see a
purple jeep. Jesse? No, it can't be. Of course it can't.
But those dusty windows and that perfect iris purple.
No, I can't even be thinking like that - Jesse
drowned in the sea. I press on the car keys and glare
as the lights blink. I step inside. I can't believe it-
this is Jesse. I'm sure of it. Or I'd like to believe it
is. Maybe it's my mind tricking me, maybe not.
There's this fragrance. It's just like her. It's a
homey, warm fragrance but light and airy at the
same time. I step inside and decide to ask Myla,
(when I get there), where she got this car, after all,
she's the one who gave me the keys.

I buckle my seatbelt, and turn the engine on with
the twist of the wrist. My new Jesse roars awake.
I'm so sure it's her, but I know that's impossible,
right? Oh, Jesse… just as I start to leave, I find a
series of letters and postcards on the passenger seat.
I pick up one of the letters and begin to read it:

"Allen,

*I'm so sorry. I wish it hadn't happened. But it had to
happen. I had to. I had to push you out. I wanted to
forget you. I needed to forget you. Because you ruined me.*

But the truth is, it wasn't your fault. Or maybe it was.

*You always admired all your success, all your passions,
your goals. You made me remember I had none. Which is
exactly why my family was more proud of you than they
have ever been of me. As you story-told with starry eyes.*

*You only needed me when you had to cope. Or blamed
me because of your coping. I can't handle it anymore. I
can't. And I'm sorry. I'm weak.*

I've read this before. I had found it- under
Griffin's bed. I remember. I pick up another letter,
and notice a phone under it. It's Pierre's phone, I
recall glimpsing at his messages questioning who he
was talking to outside of the hotel. Yet, here it is, the
phone. With the very same messages still vivid on
the screen. What does this mean? What's going on? I
hastily scramble through the objects on the seat and
under the many postcards and Pierre's phone; there's
also the bandana and the knife.

Why do I have all this stuff? Unless…

Were these cards, these letters - those 'private'
conversations planted? Was it I, who was part of an
'experiment'? Was I the one being tested …tested on
my level of loyalty? Of how far I'd go for him, for
Allen? For someone besides myself?

My head starts spinning. I gape down at the
objects in front of me and I can't decide what to
believe. I'm so confused right now. I feel like my
life has been a lie, as if I wasn't the one living it. It's
like- like I built up an entire prison just to lock
myself in it.

Now, I pick up a postcard with the image of a city
night. The sky's an innocent listener, as the ground
below cheers and laughs. The warm lights almost
seem to flicker, coming from mini apartments, along
with bejeweled bridges, occupied cars… I just
imagine everyone's different story, diverse life but

as a whole, it all seems so peaceful and picture perfect. In the lower part of the postcard, steam crawls out the manholes, probably because of an underground subway. I look at the entire postcard once more and it's like I can almost feel the cold on my cheeks, smell it too.

Such endless opportunities.

I turn it round only to skim over another fake card, a false writing to keep me immune to the truth. There are over ten unread letters and five other postcards, which had been placed for me to find. Which I hadn't found. Till now.

This strange feeling chains my neck and rattles my brain, squeezing my heart. I can't- I won't believe I've been living this lie. This test. Questions pour into my mind like stars in a night sky. Did Myla put Allen up to this? To get back at me for being an insufficient father? Or better, to see if I've changed like I said I did that day at the market? To test whether or not I've restarted caring for others again?

Allen's friends must've known about this. They were the 'actors', they tricked me into believing that *they* were the ones being tested, not me. Not I.

I was supposed to be a witness of this scheme not the victim.

My deal with Myla consisted of Allen using the hotel, to see if his friends loved him. To see how his friends would react to a fraction of pain, compared to the immense pain they put him through, during the years. It was a test for his friends, and his friends only. It was something I'd normally wouldn't allow, but I went against my own beliefs in order to show

Myla how much I'd do for her. How much I want her to trust me again, to give me another chance. To show her I've changed. I did it all for her. She's my last hope to be happy again. And she does this. She tests me. She'd never meant any of her words that day at the market, she'd just wanted to test me all along, even before I could show her I'd changed. She'd just wanted to test me, the whole time? It feels unreal. She'd tested me. Not anyone else. Just *me*.

I didn't sign up for this and it hurts, it hurts like I've been slammed into a sincerity wall. How could I have been so foolish? It felt so good to remove some of my trust off my back and give it to someone else. Lend it even. But I knew better than to have done so.

Myla has tested me. My own grandson, Allen has tested me. His friends have tested me… and I passed their test. All of their tests. I showed her, and Allen, and his friends that I'm worthy. I'm worthy of being trusted. I'm worthy of receiving another chance. And I'm capable of caring for others. I'm capable of changing.

I unlatch my seatbelt, which I still had on, and waddle out of the jeep. And- I find her standing there. Myla. In her blouse and long skirt. Her shadow elongated behind her body. She's tearing up, as a few words escape her mouth:

"I'm sorry."

And all I want to do, is what I've wanted to do for so long and it's exactly what I did: I embraced her, with my arms open wide.

'...*but my actions finalize all.*'
-Allen